# OUTLAWS:
## Ride Tall or Hang High

*Also by Chet Cunningham
in Large Print:*

Aztec Gold
Battle Cry
Bloody Gold
Boots and Saddles
Comanche Massacre
Devil's Gold
Die of Gold
Fort Blood
Gold Wagon
Renegade Army
Sioux Showdown
Sioux Slaughter

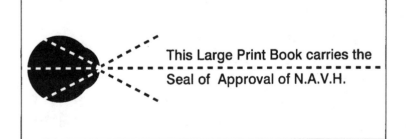

This Large Print Book carries the
Seal of Approval of N.A.V.H.

# OUTLAWS:
## Ride Tall or Hang High

*Chet Cunningham*

**Thorndike Press • Waterville, Maine**

Published in 2002 by arrangement with Chet Cunningham.

Thorndike Press Large Print Western Series.

The tree indicium is a trademark of Thorndike Press.

The text of this Large Print edition is unabridged.
Other aspects of the book may vary from the original edition.

Set in 16 pt. Plantin.

Printed in the United States on permanent paper.

**Library of Congress Cataloging-in-Publication Data**

Cunningham, Chet.
  Ride tall or hang high / Chet Cunningham.
    p. cm. — (Outlaws ; 1)
    ISBN 0-7862-4466-6 (lg. print : hc : alk. paper)
    1. Outlaws — Fiction.  2. Large type books.  I. Title.
  PS3553.U468 R53 2002
  813′.54—dc21                                    2002020486

# OUTLAWS:
## Ride Tall or Hang High

# Chapter One

*July 14, 1869: Oak Park, Texas:*

Willy Boy sat on the bottom bunk and spoke sharply to the huge man who sat beside him in the Oak Park jail cell.

"Damn right it'll work, Gunner. Would I tell you it would work if it wouldn't? Hell, no! When I go into my act and pretend I've hung myself, you yell your head off and call for the deputy. Can't be more than one out there in the office now. You scream and yell and when he comes in do what he says, then I'll grab his gun and we'll be out of here damn quick."

Gunner was six-four, a solid, big man who weighed 250 hard muscled pounds. His dark eyes peered at Willy Boy from a face that had been described as simple but Gunner wasn't slow witted, he was just a little confused at times.

Willy Boy put the noose around his neck. He had made it from his spare shirt, and tied one end on the double deck bunk frame over his head. He tested it, let the knot pull tight around his throat, pushed his tongue out so it lolled over his cheek. Then he winked and nodded at Gunner.

"Now, Gunner, call him now!" Willy Boy wheezed.

Gunner screamed for the deputy. He took off his boot and pounded on the bars with it.

"Deputy! Deputy, come quick! Willy Boy back here's in trouble. Dear God come quick, deputy!"

Across the aisle between the two rows of cells, two more men woke up and bellowed in anger at the noise. Soon the whole cell area was roaring with sound and five men were shaking their cell bars and screaming.

Deputy Sheriff Seth Matthews opened the door into the cell block cautiously. He looked in and checked see that everyone was in a cell, then he pushed his six-gun back in his holster.

"What the hell's going on?" he bellowed over the roar.

Gunner bellowed just as loud. "Willy Boy . . . he's hung himself!"

Deputy Matthews took half a dozen steps between the cells and stared at Willy Boy. His face was blue, his tongue lolling out, the whole weight of his body was on a shirt noose around his neck. He had slid off the bottom bunk and by-god was hanging himself.

"Little bastard! Should just let you die!" Deputy Matthews yelled. "We been having nothing but trouble from you, Willy Boy, since you came here two weeks ago. Hell, you claim you're only seventeen but you been charged with murder." Deputy Matthews stared at him. "Then, you bastard, you laughed and bragged about the killing."

Deputy Matthews swore. "You little shit, Willy Boy. I can't let you die on me during my guard duty shift. You don't get off that easy!"

Deputy Matthews moved over to the cell door. "Stand back, Gunner!" he barked.

Matthews took the key ring from his pocket and turned the big lock with one hand as he pulled his six-gun with the other. "Gunner, you lay down flat on your face on the floor over there. Move!"

Gunner did. He didn't like Matthews.

When Gunner was down, Matthews pushed the cell door inward and stepped toward Willy Boy. "Damn, his face is blue already, must be dead."

He knew he had to lift Willy Boy up to the bottom bunk or he'd never get the noose off his head. He tried pushing him, but it didn't work. At last he bellied up to him, put his arms around the youth's waist and hoisted him up.

As he did he felt something, a slight movement. Then he realized it was his piece. He dropped Willy Boy but already the inmate had yanked the deputy's six-gun out and lifted it to his head. Deputy Matthews saw only a flash of Willy Boy's face as he grinned and fired the .45 at point blank range.

Deputy Seth Matthews slammed backward against the outside of the cell and slid to the floor. Willy looped the shirt sleeve off his neck grinning.

"Damn! Gunner, told you it would work!" His eyes looked around the cell, then at Gunner. "Come on, Gunner. We're getting out of this damn crackerbox of a jail. Get his keys and open the other cell doors. All of them."

"Six of us in here. Six is a lot harder to hunt down than just two. We get guns at the door and nobody can stop us."

"Okay, you bastards, we're making a jailbreak. We've got one gun, and there are half a dozen more in the office out front. Gunner's gonna open up them cells, so get on your boots and get ready to travel."

"Get me a gun and I'm with you," the Professor said.

Willy Boy laughed. "No damn time to argue. We'll get a dozen guns." He went to the end of the cells. "Open them, Gunner. Everybody steps out with boots on and we all go to the front office. Either go with us or I shoot you in the head right here. Make up your mind."

He glared at the end cell where a small Mexican man sat. "Come on Juan, moving time or dead time."

Juan hesitated. "I want no part in killing lawmen," he said.

"Good, then you're dead." Willy Boy lifted the revolver and thumbed back the hammer. Juan shrugged, stepped into the aisle and walked toward the door.

The Professor was already waiting there. Willy Boy looked at Eagle who sat on his bunk. "Come on, Chief, we can use you to help us live off the land. You damn Indians are good at that."

Eagle, a full blooded Comanche, laughed softly. "I dream of getting out of jail, but not by killing a guard. If I go with you I'll be wanted for murder."

"So what?" Willy snorted. "You stay and you're one more dead Indian. Decide." Willy Boy lifted the revolver.

11

Eagle jumped off the bunk and darted down the hall to the door that had not been opened yet.

Johnny Joe Williams was out of his cell as soon as the door opened. He waited at the door. Willy Boy crowded past them and tested the door. Not locked. He opened it an inch. It came inward. He could hear nothing past it. He pulled it inward another foot and listened, then looked out.

No sounds came from the next room. He remembered it was a kind of questioning room, with a long table and chairs. Beyond that was the front office. It had windows.

He opened the next door and looked out. No one was there. He checked again, then ran through the open door to the gun rack on the far wall. It had a chain through the rifle and shotgun trigger guards.

Willy Boy grabbed the key ring and hunted for the right one but didn't find it. He shrugged, lifted the deputy's .45 and shot twice at the chain at the side of the cabinet. It broke. There were three shotguns and three rifles. They took them all.

He opened drawers until he found boxes of shells. He gave each man a box of both kinds. In another drawer he found four handguns that had been confiscated. There were .44 and .45's. Willy Boy handed them around and saw that the men loaded them.

The Professor found more pistol ammunition, and handed out boxes of it.

"Company!" Johnny Joe Williams said pointing toward the outside door that led to the street.

Almost at the same time a man came through the door into the office. He wore a tin star and saw the inmates. In a half second, his right hand darted to his hip where it clawed for his revolver.

Willy Boy already had his six-gun up and shot the deputy through the heart.

"Grab his gunbelt and pistola," Willy Boy shouted. "Damn, I got me two lawmen already and the day is just starting!"

They looked around the office, saw nothing else they could use and moved over to the door.

"We get outside, find horses and then stay together. We can fight off a damn posse this way," Willy Boy had told them this three or four times before he let anyone outside. Then he went first and told them to drift out one at a time.

Willy Boy carried a loaded shotgun as he walked out of the jail house door. Across the street a saloon was dark and quiet. From around a corner three stores down on the far side of the street, the third deputy on duty was checking store doors.

He saw one man leave the jail door in the shadows, then a second. He ran forward, his six-gun out.

Beside Willy Boy, Gunner brought up his shotgun and triggered it. One barrel of 10 gauge double-ought buck blasted forward and hit the man who was now less than 20 feet from them. The shot nearly cut him in half.

Willy Boy laughed. "Great shot, Gunner. Knew you had the right name. We get horses off the street. Check in front of saloons."

Willy Boy heard a door slam and a window close.

"Go back to sleep, you bastards!" he screamed.

Another window closed quickly. Willy Boy laughed.

Now all six of them were out of the jail. They ran down Main Street, and soon found six horses that had been left on the street in front of saloons or hotels. Drunks who forgot them, or late arrivals at the hotel who were too tired to put the mounts in the livery.

They mounted and rode out of town to the west.

"We stick together or we die singly," Willy Boy yelled at them again. "Anybody know this area? Are there any farms or ranches out this way?"

"A ranch about three, four miles out," Juan Romero said. "I worked there one summer."

"Good, let's pay them a visit. We need some food and better horses if they got them. Hey, you guys, you're free. No more hangman hovering there in the background waiting to stretch your necks, right?"

He fired the pistol in the air once and laughed again, then they rode west down the stage road. When it turned north they kept going west on a wagon track.

The Professor rode up beside Willy Boy. The Professor was the oldest one of the six. He was twenty-four and had once gone to college for a year and taught school for two years in Illinois. He was five-eleven, slender and dressed well when he could afford it. He preferred fancy gambler type vests and ruffled shirts.

"Willy Boy, I've known you for only a week, but I must admit you do have a forceful personality. However, even you can't keep these six men together against

15

their wills. Don't you think it would be better, strategically, if we let the Indian and the Mexican go on their way? Then any posse would have to split its forces to follow the three different trails."

"You talk all pretty and proper, but your ideas ain't worth shit, Professor. You ever been chased by a posse? Bunch of damn civilians who don't know one end of a rifle from the other. This damn sheriff is gonna be waking men up soon as he hears we blasted three of his deputies. He'll be mad and do crazy things trying to find us.

"Six of us fighting together can outgun him and rattle him more than one or two of us. That way we send him home without even sniffing our backsides. Besides, he might not even get out of bed until daylight. Depends on who reports the gunfire on the streets. We got some time."

Johnny Joe Williams slid into place riding on the other side of Willy Boy. The seventeen year old self appointed leader of the fugitives looked at him. "Johnny Joe, what the hell you think about what the Professor said?"

"He's right, but so are you. Right now I vote with you. You had the nerve and the guts to get us out. How did you make your face turn blue that way?"

"Held my breath. Been doing that since I was a kid. Damn fool deputy. Where you from, Johnny Joe? Never knew much about you."

"Missouri. Been making my living with the pasteboards. I've traveled most of the west since a quick job as a lawman. They tried to hang me for murder."

Willy Boy chuckled. "I think I've heard of you, Johnny Joe. Don't you have something of a reputation as a gunfighter?"

"I've been known to take up a revolver now and again. But it's a 50/50 bet and that goes against my religion. When it comes to winning, I'm highly religious."

Willy Boy roared with laughter.

He looked around, spotted the Indian close behind.

"Eagle, how far can we go west this way before we run into a whole passel of Indians?"

"Fifty miles. No camps around this area."

Willy Boy frowned at the red man. "Hear you was in jail for cutting up one of the deputies. You kill some white eyes or you just hurt him bad?"

Eagle snorted. "I didn't even start to hurt the sheriff when three more of them arrived. This town had too many deputies. But it don't have quite so many now."

Willy Boy laughed again.

Juan Romero rode up and motioned for them to turn to the left. "The ranch is about half a mile down this trail. I don't even know if anyone is living there now."

"Romero, you were waiting trial for knifing some cowboy. I hear he started it and it was a fair fight and he cut you, but you're the one they arrested."

"*Sí*. I made the mistake of cutting the mayor's drunken son and the mayor charged me."

Willy Boy nodded. "Happens, Juan. The law just ain't equal to everybody, especially Mexicans in Texas. That's why the six of us is gonna even it up a little here and there and around the edges. You know how lawmen are always killing the bad guys? Well, tonight the bad guys evened it up a little with three sheriff's deputies down and dead."

They could see the outlines of the ranch ahead. There were no lights. Ten minutes later they found that the place was deserted. Inside the small ranch house they discovered an old cook stove and two beds that had been left behind with some other furniture. Somebody had left in a rush.

Willy Boy looked over the house. It was sturdily built. Rifle bullets wouldn't go through the wooden sides. Two windows

18

were already broken out.

"Let's park it here for the rest of the night. I'll be on guard until daylight, then I want a volunteer as the rest of us get some sleep."

Eagle held up his hand.

Willy Boy watched him a minute.

"Maybe this is a good time to say it. I got you all out of jail. Wasn't for me and my little act and my gun, every one of you would be back there still. I saved some of you from getting hung or at least 20 years in prison. Nobody leaves this bunch until I say so. Anybody leaves, I track him down and blow his damn head off. Everybody got that straight? Now is the time to talk it out."

He waited a minute. No one said anything. "Good. Now, let's get our horses put away in the barn out there, but leave them saddled. We might have to leave sudden. Then the rest of you get some sleep."

He grinned. "Don't worry, Willy Boy is here to take care of you all."

# Chapter Two

*Willy Boy* let the men settle down in the house. They had no blankets, no bedrolls or camping gear and no food. They'd hit the first ranch they came to and pick up needed supplies — courtesy of the rancher.

When the sprawled men slept, Willy Boy took a Spencer Carbine and a box of .52 caliber shells and climbed into the barn. The haymow door had been left swung down and he sat there 15 feet off the ground staring out the opening. It was a good lookout spot since he could see halfway back to town in that flat part of the Texas panhandle.

He grinned to himself thinking about the night's work. Hell, he hadn't asked to be put in that damn little jail or to be tried and convicted of that damn dumb killing. So he had to get out. He had always done just about what he needed to do.

He chuckled about pretending to be hanged. If that damn deputy wasn't so dumb he'd be alive. He should have used a knife and cut down the shirt rope. That

20

would have accomplished the same thing. No, he had to come in close and lift.

And then the six of them rode away on those *borrowed* horses. He didn't expect a posse before daylight, if then. First they'd have to try to find some tracks. They could have gone in any of four directions. Should they push on and find a ranch and some food and gear next? Willy Boy thought about it a moment and decided. He liked to do everything quick. Yeah, they'd find a ranch.

Hell, he had his own gang now. The Professor was a cool one, good with a gun and smart, smartest man in the bunch. He was looking at 20 years in prison. He'd be with the group forever. Good old Gunner was just a bit slow in his thinking, but he was Willy Boy's slave for life. Just took one or two times sticking up for Gunner and the big man now prayed on the ground where Willy Boy walked.

Johnny Joe Williams, the gambler. He'd stick with them at least until they got out of Texas. Johnny Joe was a gambler and right now this was a better hand than the ten year sentence the judge as well as told him he'd get.

The question marks were Eagle and the Mex. Eagle would come in damn handy out in the open and on the run. He was full blooded Comanche, would know this country and how to live off the land if they had to. He knew the Indian was kill-mad at the army. His family had tried to surrender to an army company and they waded in and killed everyone in sight. Eagle was only ten or twelve at the time and they hauled him off to a mission school where he learned English and how to read and write.

Eagle would want to go after Able Troop in the Fourteenth Cavalry Regiment sooner or later.

Juan Romero, the Mex. Now there could be a problem. He was in jail for a simple knifing. Juan had never ridden the owlhoot trail, never been on the run from the law. But he would come around. Now he could be charged with murder; that would keep him in line for a time. He could be valuable if they decided to swing down into Mexico to outrun some posse.

Being raised in western Missouri, Willy Boy's Spanish lingo wasn't too good. Juan would be invaluable down there. For just a moment Willy Boy thought about his father. His fist drew the six-gun from his belt and he waved it at the barn roof. His fingers went white on the gun butt as he gripped it.

"Goddamn the bastard!" Willy Boy said softly. "I'm gonna find the sombitch and kill him slow, like the Comanches do. He'll be sorry as hell he ever gunned down my pa!"

The damn bounty hunter had blown Hartley Lambier right out of his shoes as soon as he opened the door to their little farm house. Never a howdy, not a question about what his name was, or nothing. Just a sawed off shotgun blast from four feet.

The tall, thin Texan had stormed into the house and looked at his victim's face and his bright red hair and he swore. He'd killed the wrong man. He looked around the cabin and saw Willy Boy who was nearly fourteen. The bounty hunter shook his head and lifted his sawed off scatter gun and fired the second round.

Willy Boy had been fast even then. He saw it coming and dove behind an old dresser which took the slugs, then busted out a window and ran screaming and bleeding into the night where the killer could never find him. He'd seen the bounty hunter around the little town of Leaverville. Willy Boy heard tell he was a famous bounty man called Deeds Conover.

There were only he and his pa on the

little farm. His ma had been taken two years before by the consumption. Willy Boy had run half the night to be sure he was away from Deeds Conover. The next day Willy Boy came back and got his dad's old .44 and his gunbelt and strapped them on.

From that day to this he'd been looking for Deeds Conover. But he'd had trouble since the first. In Kansas City a drunk tried to rob him and Willy Boy shot him, killed the man and they arrested him. It wasn't right, the drunk had a gun too and was grabbing for it.

A week later, Willy Boy pretended to be sick with a blue face and no breath. He broke out of jail when the doctor came to help him. In the process he killed a guard, took his gun and gun belt and his horse and lit out of town for Texas.

That was three years ago, and he hadn't been in jail since, until he hit Oak Park. Twice he'd been on the trail of Deeds Conover, but each time the man moved fast and got away. Maybe the third time would be the charm.

Willy Boy stood and stared back toward the little town of Oak Park. He couldn't see the lights, nor could he hear any horses pounding their way along the trail. They'd wait until morning now, Willy guessed. By then Willy Boy and his gang would be gone. He looked at the moon, then the big dipper and figured the time. Maybe two more hours to sunrise. He could sleep in the saddle. The important thing now was to get moving. He wanted to be properly set up before he had to stand and fight against the posse he was sure would be coming after them come daylight.

Juan should know where there was another rancher around here. He was local.

Willy Boy grinned when he thought of the way he had engineered the jail break. He was good. He could do it all. He had five men to back him now and nothing could stop him from finding and killing Deeds Conover.

He wasn't the least bit sleepy. He knew he was running on the excitement of the break. Sometimes he had stayed up without sleep for three full days, and he had been as sharp and quick the third day as the first.

With the first touches of light in the sky he went and took one long last look toward town, saw nothing, and crawled down to rouse the men.

The Professor was sitting up watching

the dawn when Willy Boy walked in. He smoked a thick, brown cigar and waved.

"So far, no pursuit. I'd guess about noon."

Willy Boy nodded, shook the other four awake.

He squatted down in front of Juan. "We need a farm or a ranch where we can get some food, maybe some more guns. Any ideas?"

"The Galloways got a ranch about six, seven miles north."

"They friends of yours?"

"No. Wouldn't know me from anybody."

"They have a cookshack and horses?"

"Run about three hands, usually. Thirty, forty horses."

"Let's ride."

They looked toward town, then rode out, each man on a different trail as they worked across the grasslands heading north. A tracker would have a hard time figuring out what happened to all six sets of tracks.

They rode for an hour and a half, keeping a watch over their shoulders, but no dust cloud showed behind them that could herald a posse. When they topped a small rise, Juan pulled up.

"That's the spread. This family . . . these

are good people, don't have much, struggling to make a living."

"Take it easy, relax, *amigo*," Willy Boy said. "We aren't a bunch of mad killers here. We'll explain what we need and promise to send payment for it when we can. I think they'll understand."

When they rode in, a man came out of a small adobe ranch house with a double barreled shotgun over his arm, not aimed at them, just handy.

"Morning, gents," the rancher called. He was a tall man, thin and with a drooping moustache.

Willy Boy was out front and he nodded. "Morning, yourself. We was wondering maybe you could help us out. We're getting ready to travel cross country and we don't have enough supplies. Could we buy some victuals off you?"

The rancher eyed them a minute and shrugged. "Don't have a lot, but guess we could spare you some. New potatoes about due so we can use up the old ones. Got a sack of beans, and butchered out a steer last night. The wife was gonna can most of it, but we can spare a quarter."

"We thank you kindly, sir," the Professor said. "A bit down on our supplies right now. Not a good place to try to live off the fruits of the land."

"Stand down, men, and I'll have the wife pour some coffee. Always got a hot pot on the kitchen stove."

They had coffee and met his wife and two tow headed kids, then went to the root cellar and got fifty pounds of potatoes in a sack, and ten pounds of dried beans in an old flour sack.

"Could you use a pound or two of good coffee beans?" the rancher asked.

"Now that would be real neighborly of you," Willy Boy said.

The rancher looked up. "I reckon you got your own grinder."

"Had one," the Professor said. "Dang thing broke on us about two days back, had to junk it along the trail."

"I got a spare one I usually send on the chuck wagon. Them beans won't do you no good without grinding."

An hour later they had eaten slabs of fresh bread with country butter and crab apple butter on them and downed the last of the coffee. They had the food latched onto the back of saddles, and all the men mounted up but Willy Boy.

"Now, sir, what is the cost of all these goods?" Willy Boy asked.

Frank Galloway pulled at his jaw a

minute, then shook his head. "Don't rightly think you gents owe me a thing. In another month most of the spuds would be rotted. And the beans I would have taken to the church bazaar for the building fund. The beef don't cost cause I had to kill it when the dang fool steer broke a hind leg. I'd say we're about even."

Willy Boy frowned. "I don't take charity, Mr. Galloway," Willy Boy said stretching up to all of his five-feet six height.

Galloway chuckled. "No, don't rightly guess you do. Let's say if you have a spare five dollar bill over the next two or three months, you mail it to me. Name's Frank Galloway, Oak Park, Texas. I'll find it at the post office down at the general store. You boys have a good ride now, hear?"

Willy Boy held out his hand. "We thank you kindly. Fact is, we are a bit short right now. But we'll pay you." He shook the man's huge hand again, then stepped in the saddle, waved and led the five men on north.

When they were out of earshot, the Professor rode up beside Willy Boy.

"Best hand I ever seen bluffed, Willy Boy," he said.

"No bluff. I would have signed a paper for him, an I.O.U. paper."

"Then you aim to pay him?"

"Damn right. He was straight with us. First damn five dollar bill we steal, I'm gonna send to him in an envelope."

Juan came riding up beside him. He was grinning. "That *gringo,* I know him and he knows me."

"What?" Willy Boy asked.

"Sure. I didn't know that was his name. He was on the jury that convicted me. He knew who I was right away. He knew I'm supposed to be in jail."

The Professor frowned. "Put a black suit on him, comb his hair and he does come familiar. I think he was on my jury, too."

Willy Boy laughed. "Be damned. So he must have figured we busted out of jail. He also knew he was outgunned six to one and didn't want to die for the county court-house or the sheriff."

The Professor chuckled. "About the size of it. You still going to send him that five dollar bill?"

"Damned right. I'm a man of my word. I gave the man my word so he gets the fiver as soon as I can steal one."

A short time later, Willy Boy found a small rise and he brought the group to a stop. They stared back to the south the way they had come and on to the area where Oak Park, Texas, should lay.

"Nobody coming yet," Gunner said.

Willy Boy looked at him and nodded. "Not yet, but soon. What do most men do when they try to get away from a posse, Professor?"

"Run as damn fast as they can."

"Right, that's why most of them get caught. We're not going to run. We're going to fight, only the difference is we're going to pick the time and place, at least the place. That's what I'm hunting now. I want to find an ideal spot where we can lure that posse into a trap, and then cut it to pieces."

"They know that we're well armed — three shotguns, three rifles and handguns," the Professor said.

"Sure they know, but they still have to come after us. That sheriff can't let six men escape from his jail and not make a hell of a big try to get us back. If he don't, he's not going to get elected next time. He'll be here. All we need to do is find the spot and let him track us to it."

"So where's the spot?" Eagle asked.

Willy Boy turned to the Comanche. "Eagle, you're our outdoor expert, where is the best place for an ambush around here?"

Eagle stood in his stirrups and stared around the land. At last he pointed to the west. "Some small hills over there two or three miles. We find a little valley and build a camp in it, then get on the sides of the ridges and attack them when they storm into the camp. We have a good crossfire."

"Eagle, damn glad you decided to come along. Any idea where the Cavalry Fourteenth Regiment is posted?"

Eagle looked up sharply. He shook his head.

"Don't worry, my new friend. We'll find them before we're through. Right now let's go over to those hills and look at the lay of the land."

A half hour later Willy Boy grinned. He sat on his horse on a ridge 50 yards high. Another one about the same size loomed across the narrow valley. Between them a small stream flowed bordered by a strip of brush and a few live oaks and large pecan trees. There was plenty of room where they could set up a camp.

"Damn, we don't have any blanket rolls," Willy Boy said. He shrugged. "We'll get some first store we come by, whether we have any cash or not."

Willy Boy looked at the other five who nodded.

"Looks good," the Professor said.

"Seems made to order, but I wish we had four more rifles," Johnny Joe said.

"Let's get down there and make a camp just tempting as all hell," Willy Boy ordered. They all rode down into the valley.

# Chapter Three

A *million* harpies beat their big wings at him and a thousand of them screamed in his ears setting his head on fire, the thundering sounds dulling his other senses until he figured he was half dead, but through it all came a white hot anger that little by little forced the harpies away and the sounds to fade until it was nothing more than a pounding headache which sounded through his skull like a thousand hoof beats.

When he tried to open his eyes the whole world was black, and when his hands touched the floor it was sticky. He pushed himself up to a sitting position, moving slowly so his head wouldn't explode right off his shoulders. At last he could make out the faint outline of the windows, high up with bars on them.

Sticky, what was so damn wet?

What in hell was he doing back in the block of jail cells?

Slowly he remembered. That damn Willy Boy. That goddamned Willy Boy! He had been damn near dead, hanging that way in his bunk, his throat held by a tight noose of cloth, body suspended, his face as blue as the sky and his tongue lolling out . . .

That's when Deputy Seth Matthews remembered. Willy Boy had grabbed his gun and shot him in the head. So he must be dead. The problem was that he hurt too damn much to be dead. They must have blown out the lamp usually left burning in the jail cell corridor.

Seth knew he had to get out of there, out to the front. Willy Boy must be gone.

"Anybody . . ." The sound of his voice came blasting into his head and he closed his eyes and let a spasm of pain gush through touching every one of his million sensitive nerve points.

"Anybody here?" he said on the second try.

Silence. He had to do it himself. Willy Boy must have cleaned out the jail, all six prisoners gone and it was his own god-damn fault.

Seth tried to get his feet under him. Sticky, slippery. How much did he bleed anyway? He grabbed the bunk and got on his knees, then a minute later he got one foot under him. When he tried to heave upward he almost blacked out.

"Christ, I might as well be dead," he said softly. Then he tried again, got his second foot under him without standing. Slowly he came from his squatting position upright gripping the top bunk as he worked up gradually.

"Made it, by damn!"

He shuffled carefully to the end of the bunk, then teetered until he got across the three feet to the cell door and into the aisle. It took him another five minutes to work his way slowly to the door of the midroom, then on to the office.

There at least a lamp still burned. At once he saw a body sprawled beside the front door, just inside. He could tell it was Deputy Chris Gerber by the side of his head. A pool of blood under his chest told a deadly story.

Seth automatically felt for his six-gun.

Gone. Still had the belt. He looked at the gunrack. Empty. Goddamn. Six escaped prisoners. Three set to be hung, three to go to prison soon.

He got to the front door with the last of his strength and pushed it open. Seth had no idea what time it was. Still dark out. He checked but didn't see anyone on the street. Not a chance he could walk the block and a half to Sheriff Dunwoody's house. Anyway, there were four steps up to the front door. He'd never make them.

Seth felt his strength slipping away. He couldn't even fire some shots to attract attention. He leaned against the wall of the jail and slid down the wall to a sitting position. Somebody would be out and around early, see him, call the sheriff. Somebody.

Seth tried to stay awake. He was afraid if he went to sleep he'd die. But he was so tired. His head thundered again, blasting at him with deadly throbbing pain. He must have lost a lot of blood, too. How much could a man lose and not die? He didn't know. Head wound, he could feel it now. And smell the singed hair. Powder burns, too, hurt like hell. Head wound, lots of blood, not much damage, but enough. Paid to have a thick skull, told his wife that a thousand times.

Damn him, damn Willy Boy! Killed Gerber. Where was the other man on duty, the new one, Bowden? Why wasn't he here? As the mists of sleep and unconsciousness closed in on him, Seth realized that Bowden must be dead, too, or wounded. If Bowden wasn't down he'd be at the jail, he would have found Seth. Damn.

That Willy Boy, damn him.

"I'll get you, Willy Boy. I'll get you if it's the last goddamn thing I ever do."

The pledge made, Deputy Sheriff Seth Matthews of Oak County, let his head roll to the right and drifted off to sleep.

"Seth! Seth, wake up! Good God, are you dead, too? Seth?"

"What? Huh?" Seth came back to reality as someone shook his shoulder. He blinked and worked the fog out of his eyes and looked up.

"Oh, God, that hurts!" Seth bleated.

Sheriff Dunwoody knelt beside him on the boardwalk.

"Seth, what happened? Jail's open, the prisoners are gone. I got two dead deputies and you look worse than dead."

Doc Farnham scurried up with his little black bag and knelt on the boardwalk.

"Now, this one I can do something for." He looked at Seth's head and came back in front of him. "Seth, now you can tell everyone that you've been shot in the head. Bullet tore the skin and scalp off your head a quarter of an inch wide, but never did much damage. I'll wager you think it nigh killed you."

"No jokes, Doc. Hurts enough to kill me."

"Powder burns'll be what's hurting the most. Burned off some hair, blistered your scalp. You'll wear a hat for a while. Lots of blood on a hurt like this."

"Doc, he's gonna be all right?" Sheriff Dunwoody asked.

"Good as new in a few days, minus a little hair."

"Seth, who did this?"

"Willy Boy. Tricked me. Hung himself on his bunk. Face all blue, tongue lolling out, not breathing. I put Gunner down on the floor then went in the cell. Tried to lift him off the noose. Then he grabbed my gun and shot me."

"We don't even know which way they went," the sheriff said. "You know all six of them got away?"

"I'll be ready to go on the posse in an hour, Sheriff," Seth said.

"Not a chance. You get over to Doc's and get patched up. Come back in two days. The day crew'll be here at seven. We'll put a posse together. Any guess which way they might go?"

Seth started to shake his head but it hurt too much.

"I'll send out a tracker to make a circle around town soon as I can find somebody. We'll get a posse together to leave about nine. Damn! We got to get them men back. Two of them are scheduled to hang next week!"

By nine that morning, Sheriff Jim Dunwoody led out his posse of 25 men. All were getting a dollar a day from the county and all brought their own rifles and pistols, their bedrolls and enough food for five days.

Before they left, Sheriff Dunwoody talked to them. "Men, this won't be the usual one day posse. I figure these men will run long and hard. We might not even catch them for three days. When we do, they have rifles and shotguns and we know they'll fight. Hell, three of them been sentenced to hang, so they have nothing to lose. Anyone who doesn't want to go on that kind of a ride better back off right now."

He waited and two men changed their minds and rode out of the group.

"All right, we still have 24 of us all together. Our tracker has given us a direction. They headed out toward the old Paulson ranch. Let's get moving."

Deputy Seth Matthews sat in Doc Farnham's office and watched out the window as they rode away. "Watch out for that little bastard," Seth mumbled. "He's a killer, nothing but a goddamned killer."

Sheriff Dunwoody rode at the head of the posse the way he always did. He was 41 years old, tough as old leather and worked at keeping fit. He rode every day and could shoot with the best of them. In his boot he carried a Spencer repeater and a Blakeslee Quickloader from the army with 13 tubes filled with 7 rounds of .52 caliber each for the Spencer.

He carried on his hip an 1860 Army Percussion Revolver bored out to take solid cartridges in the .44 caliber. It had an 8-inch barrel and he claimed that on two shots out of three he could hit a man at 40 yards with it.

The posse wasted no time at the vacant Paulson ranch. Their scout and tracker, who rode ahead of the main party, waved them on past when they came to it. The scout, Adolph K. Scoggins, rode back and talked with the sheriff.

"They heading on north. Won't find six tracks anywhere, they're trying to be cute, splitting up into six trails, but I cut all six of them riding north."

"What's up there, Adolph?"

"Six or seven miles out there's a three-hand little ranch. Forget the guy that owns it. But as I remember, he was one of the men on the jury who found at least one of the fugitives guilty."

"Could be a bloody scene we find. Let's pick up the pace," the sheriff said.

Adolph went on out to scout the trail and the sheriff lifted the riders to a trot for two miles, then eased off.

They found the Frank Galloway ranch a little before noon. The place hadn't been burned down. The sheriff and scout rode in and Frank Galloway came out of the barn with a pitchfork.

"Figured you'd be along before now," Frank said.

"They was here?"

"Yeah, they were here," Frank said. "You just tracked them in. We fed them some coffee and some bread and jam and they moved on north," Frank said and grinned. "Looks like somebody cleaned out that whole damn jail of yours, Sheriff Dunwoody."

"Looks that way. They know you was a juryman?"

"Might. If so, they didn't say nothing. Offered to pay for some food they wanted."

"They get it?"

"Damn right. I know when I'm outgunned. They asked nice like. If I'd said no, I'd probably be dead now, and you'd have three or four graves to dig."

"Yeah, probably. Watch your hindside with them six on the loose. They might remember you was one sentenced them to hang."

The posse swung north with the tracker finding the six fugitives all riding together again.

"They stayed what was left of the night at the first ranch, left about daylight, I'd guess," Scoggins told the sheriff. "Which puts us about three, maybe three and a half hours behind them."

"Nothing much else up this way is there?"

"Indian Territories another thirty, forty miles," the scout said. "Couple of small towns, nothing to speak of."

"So where the hell they going?"

"The Territories. Place where lots of wanted men go. Nobody wants to go in there after them but a few U.S. Marshalls."

"We'll go in. I can't face the judge if they all get away. Strange how they keep together this way. Usually six men running from a posse will take off six different ways."

"This gives you a chance to catch all six at once," Scoggins said.

"Also gives them six times the firepower if it comes down to a firefight."

They kept quiet then and pushed ahead a little faster. The land was mostly flat grasslands here, with a small rise now and then and two miles to the front some low hills.

"Smoke ahead," the scout reported to the sheriff when they were about a mile from the hills.

"Smoke, I don't see any," the lawman said.

"Neither do I, Sheriff. But you should be able to smell it. Figure they must have decided they were away clean and settled down to a camp and cook some of the grub they got off Galloway back there."

"Possible. If so, we should slip up on them easy like. Ride out front and see what you can figure on them."

When the scout came back he was grinning.

"Be damned, Sheriff, you must be living right. I got within a quarter mile of the place. They holed up in a little valley between some ridges. It has a creek and they've built up a good sized fire. I spotted at least three horses in the brush. Fire's in behind a thicket I couldn't see through. Also know something else.

"Somebody down there is cooking some beef. Smell comes through good enough to eat. We've got them!"

Sheriff Dunwoody grinned. "By damn, I think we have." He turned to his Deputy Kenny. "Keep the men here, out of sight, and keep them quiet. No smoking or gunfire."

He turned to Scoggins, the scout. "Take me up there where you were. I want to check out the situation."

Twenty minutes later Sheriff Dunwoody bellied down in the grass and looked across at the little valley. "Now I can smell that beef cooking. Yes, I see horses, two at least. The fire is just behind that heavy brush."

"Sheriff, we could get on the little ridges on both sides and pour fire in there and kill everything alive."

"Might, might not. We got to be sure it's them. Could be a couple of rawhiders in there or some sodbuster family with six kids looking for a farm. That'd be a hell of a note killing them kids. We got to be sure. We ride in with guns up and ready and when we see it's the fugitives, we let loose. We'll go in like the cavalry, a company front all stretched out in a line so nobody shoots our own men."

A half hour later the posse was lined up and ready to go.

"No shooting until we're sure these are the jailbirds," Sheriff Dunwoody admonished. "Then we blast anybody who moves or shoots back. I'll give the order to fire. Nobody shoots before I do, is that clear?" The riders all nodded.

Sheriff Dunwoody took his place in the center of the line and they came up over the small rise and into the valley. Now the 24 riders were in full view of the brushy camp but there was no sign they had been seen. They moved ahead at a walk. When they were 100 yards from the brush and still nothing had happened, Sheriff Dunwoody whistled and waved forward with his hand and spurred his mount into a gallop.

Twenty seconds later the horses crashed through the brush around the camp and the men saw the fire and the two horses but no men.

"Oh, Christ!" Sheriff Dunwoody said just before the first rifle fire came from both of the ridges.

# Chapter Four

Willy Boy had put two of the riflemen on the west ridge and one on the east. Eagle had been placed down in the brush along the stream 50 feet up from the fake outlaws' camp. He held a piece of string in each hand. The string stretched 30 feet down the creek to where they had tied two of the shotguns firmly onto a cottonwood tree.

All four of the barrels were aimed at the small campsite. It was left up to Eagle just when to pull the string that would set off the shotguns. One pull on each gun would fire one barrel, another pull would set off the second round from each deadly weapon.

Eagle lay in the brush well out of the firing lines and watched the posse boil around near the camp in total confusion. The rifle rounds from both sides had sent two riders into panic and they galloped downstream.

He saw four of the riders shot off their horses. Six of the mounted men started upstream.

Eagle pulled one string in each hand and full loads of double-ought buck from each shotgun blasted toward the six riders. Three of them went off their saddles, screaming on the ground. Two of the other riders' horses took massive hits from the .32 caliber sized double-ought buck and bellowed as they died.

"Get out of here!" Eagle heard someone scream and the posse began falling back. Once out of the brush they rode like wild men down the little valley of death and away. The rifle fire followed them for half a mile, then tapered off.

Eagle had been in bloody battles before, but nothing like this. He lifted up from his concealed spot and walked forward slowly, his six-gun cocked and ready.

Someone moaned to the left. He looked that way and saw a man with his chest smashed in. The wounded man lifted one hand asking for help, then he died.

There were five more dead from the posse, two dead horses, and four un-claimed mounts prancing around or chomping on fresh green grass along the water.

Eagle waved his hands over his head and the other outlaws came down from the slopes.

Willy Boy ran down, his rifle in both hands as he jumped and skidded and hurried into the death scene.

"Goooooooddammmmmm!" Willy screeched. "Look at this. This was an ambush I should become famous for. Hell, we could have killed every man, but we eased off on the rifle fire. Eagle, you only fired two of the shotgun barrels. You saving the other two?"

The Professor stared at the bodies for a minute, then walked over and caught two of the horses and tied them to brush. Johnny Joe walked down the other two good horses and brought them back. Each saddle had a food sack.

"Get the food off them other two dead horses," Willy Boy said. "We'll take these four nags and see which ones we like. We'll also pick up holsters for anybody who wants one, and a new six-gun. Take a look. Should be five or six rifles here. If they have any good ones we can use at least three more."

When the men had made their selection they were fully armed. They had one more Spencer repeater, one Henry repeater, and two Springfield single shots. They took all the ammunition they could find off the bodies and dead horses.

"Gunner, look through their pockets and see if they got any cash money with them. Won't do them no good and we got to buy some more food and camping gear, pots and pans to cook with.

"Juan, get mounted up and go check on that posse. See how far they run and where they're headed. We'll meet you down at the end of the ridge in about half an hour."

When Juan left, they brought down their horses, got the two they had left as bait at the campsite, and got saddled up.

Eagle kept looking at the five pound chunk of beef roasting over the fire. The beef still hung on the green stick Eagle had set it on almost an hour ago.

"Go ahead, Eagle, bring the beef. No sense letting it go to waste. We'll get away from these flies and we can have a chew on it."

They rode out five minutes later. Eagle was careful to make sure the campfire was well put out with dirt and water from the stream.

Juan waited for them where the finger ridge melted into the grassland.

"Looks like they're headed back to town," Juan reported. "They stopped out about a half mile and bound up some gunshots, looked like. Then they kept on going."

"Think they'll be back?" Willy Boy asked.

"Damn right, they'll be back," the Professor said. "Dunwoody is a tenacious bulldog, his reputation is on the line here. He'll be back, but when he comes it will be with some dedicated professional gunmen who know what they're doing."

"So we move," Willy Boy said making the instant decision. "The question is which way, into the Indian Territories, or west into the New Mexico Territory, the badlands?"

"We need some camping gear," Juan said. "Blankets, some pots and a fry pan, knives and forks."

"Gunner how did you do back there?"

Gunner rode up beside him and fished eleven dollars out of his pocket and handed it to Willy Boy.

"That's all they had?"

Willy Boy nodded. "Thanks, Gunner." He fingered the eleven dollars a minute, then held it up. "Gentlemen, we have a total of eleven dollars. We are without funds. Does anyone have an idea how to remedy this matter so we can continue our lives as free men?"

The five looked at him.

Willy Boy scowled. "I thought we had some talent here. Isn't there an expert among us who knows how to make quick loans from banks?"

The Professor grinned. "It would seem that you're speaking about me, Willy Boy. Yes, we could make a withdrawal from a bank. But first we'd need a town. Where's the closest one that isn't Oak Park?"

"Juan, you know about this area," Willy Boy said.

"Ummmm, closest town to us would be Clayton, over the line in New Mexico, maybe fifteen miles."

Willy Boy nodded. "Let's cut up that roast beef and take a chaw on it before it spoils," he said.

They were still near the stream. Eagle washed off a large rock near the water, lay the roast beef slab on it and cut off slices with his hunting knife. The meat was cooked almost through with only a little redness in the middle.

They held the still warm roast beef slices with their fingers and ate.

"Damn good," Gunner said. They agreed. When the first slices were gone, Gunner and Juan went back for seconds. They all had a long drink of water and that reminded Willy Boy.

"We'll need canteens, too, maybe even a tent we could set up. Might as well have all the comforts since some bank is paying for it."

"Hats," Gunner said. "We don't got no hats for nobody."

Willy Boy laughed. "Damned if you ain't right. We'll get everybody the same color hat, black. That way we'll be able to spot each other easier. Now let's ride. Take that posse at least two or three days to find us. By then we'll be ready to camp or fight or go for one hell of a long ride."

They rode west the rest of the morning and most of the afternoon. By four they came in sight of a small town that Juan said was Clayton. It was a poor little town, with adobe buildings, a Catholic church, and surprisingly fair sized business district.

"A lot of farmers and ranchers from around here come into Clayton for supplies," Juan told them. "I used to work up here for a while."

They camped a mile out of town, roasted more of the beef and buried potatoes in the dirt under the fire and found them cooked after a two hour fire had the beef roasted to a turn once you got through the charred outside.

"Salt," Johnny Joe Williams said when he broke open his baked potato. "I usually want salt and pepper and lots of butter on a baked potato." He laughed. "But today this one is just right, the way it is."

"This bank," Willy Boy said licking the roast off his fingers. "Just how do we go about knocking it over?"

They all looked at the Professor.

"Bankers are like anybody else," the Professor began. "They don't like to get shot or knifed or even beaten up. So we accommodate them. We'll go in the bank, one at a time, to get change for a bill. There'll be a line when closing time comes. At three o'clock we lock the outside door, get our guns on everyone left in the bank and the tellers and bank manager. After that, it's a snap. I'll show you boys how to do it tomorrow. I've done four banks that way and never fired a shot."

"Damn, how you do that?" Willy Boy asked.

"Show you tomorrow. Now it's time for my siesta. Wanta take a little nap before I go to bed."

They let the fire die down. There was no worry about the Oak Park sheriff yet. He would be two days back by the time he got started.

Willy Boy watched each of the men. The Professor and Johnny Joe were solidly with him. Gunner was his slave for life. Eagle probably figured by now that he had found a gang that could help him get back at the army.

Juan worried Willy Boy. The young Mexican had the most to lose. He had a wife and small son somewhere. Juan said they fled back to Mexico when he was arrested. She was probably with her parents down around Guadalupe, which was downriver from El Paso. But by now, Juan was painted with the same brush as the rest of them. He was a convicted felon, he had escaped from jail where two deputies were killed and he had participated in the slaughter of six men in a posse that chased them. Juan couldn't afford to go back to Oak City. He was a fugitive and by now some printer had worked up a wanted sign on him.

He had to stay with them or run for Mexico. Willy Boy decided that he'd work on Juan, show him he appreciated his help.

As he lay there on the ground watching the sky, he figured that by the next night they would have blankets and camp gear and everything. If the robbery went right, nobody would know it happened until several hours later. That would give them time to buy what they needed and be out of town before anyone knew about the bank being gutted of all its cash.

Willy Boy grinned. Damn! This was more fun than pulling up girls' dresses. Although he could stand a little of that by now. Not tomorrow night, but soon. The next town after Clayton would do. They'd have money, and time, and there would be whores. There were always whores, everywhere.

Hats, yes, they had to have hats, but at five dollars for a good one, they would have to wait until after their coffers were filled at the cooperating bank.

Deeds Conover. Willy Boy lay with his head on his saddle, his feet to the fire, and wondered where the murderous bounty hunter was now? Willy Boy knew that he would find him. Once they shook this Oak Park posse from their trail, they would head into Kansas where he had heard that Deeds Conover usually worked. When he found the man there would be justice at last, but it would be a long and painful death for the man who shot down his father in cold blood without even asking who he was.

Most bounty hunters went after men

who were wanted dead or alive. It was a lot easier to get a sheriff to swear that a wanted man had been brought in dead over his horse, than it was to transport a live man 500 miles to collect the same sized reward.

There would be no reward for Deeds Conover. He was wanted, slowly dead, by Willy Boy. And that was what Willy Boy was going to have, soon.

The next morning they drifted into town by ones and twos, had breakfast with a dollar Willy Boy gave to each one. The biggest breakfast at the Clayton Cafe was only 35 cents. They walked the streets, picked out the places where they would leave their horses and listened one last time to the Professor.

"This is the civilized way to rob a bank," he told them. "We all have six lengths of rawhide in our pockets to tie up people, and we each have two extra bandanas to gag them with.

"If the bank has a back door, we slip out the back door and walk to where we're going, bold as we can be."

"What if there ain't no back door?" Johnny Joe asked.

"Then we come out the front door one

at a time, like the bank manager is letting us out after hours. Happens all the time. We lock the door when we leave and no one is the wiser."

"We don't get to shoot anybody?" Willy Boy asked, disappointment all over his face.

"Not unless you want me to shoot you. This is a quiet robbery. Remember, no shooting unless we have to because somebody else shoots first."

The Professor grinned. "I went into the bank a while ago. There is a back door. We'll leave our horses along the hitching rail in twos around the general store."

Willy Boy picked it up. "So we can all come out, get some money, and Juan and I will buy the cooking gear and some more food. The rest of you get your own blankets, hats, canteens, anything else you need. You'll have twenty dollars to spend."

There were no more questions. It was almost two-thirty. They walked back to Main Street and filtered along toward the bank. They had to get there at just the right time.

At five minutes until three, the Professor went into the Clayton Savings Bank. There were two tellers and a bookkeeper and in a small office a man who might be the owner, president or manager.

A teller looked up at the Professor.

"I can help you now, sir."

The Professor had a dollar bill. "I really need change for this, can you help me? My son wants all nickels. An imposition, I realize, but I would appreciate it."

As he was at the cage, two more of the gang came in, then the last three.

"Oh, dear, a rush, just at closing. Excuse me, I'll lock the door so we don't get anyone else." He locked the front door, pulled down the blind, then Willy Boy grabbed him, his six-gun in his side.

"Don't even wiggle little bank man. This is a stickup!" Willy Boy grinned as he said it.

The Professor vaulted over the waist high counter across the bank, his six-gun in hand and grabbed the bookkeeper and shoved him into the small office where a man had just reached in a drawer for a pistol.

The Professor slammed the drawer against the banker's fingers, breaking two of them.

"Just relax, everyone," Willy Boy said. "This is a bank robbery and we don't intend on killing anyone. So do what you're told and we'll all be alive to have supper."

# Chapter Five

Johnny Joe vaulted over the counter and put his revolver against the head of one remaining bank teller and told him to lay down on the floor. He did at once. He put his knee in the middle of the teller's back and quickly tied his hands and feet, then put the gag around his mouth tying it tightly in back of his neck.

By the time he had the teller tied up, all four men in the bank were tied and gagged.

Johnny Joe cleaned out the teller's cage cash drawers, looked around for more money but found none. He ran to the vault with its standing open door.

Willy Boy was there stuffing stacks of bills into canvas bank bags. The Professor did the same with a drawer filled with gold coins. They went through the vault twice, decided they had every bit of money in the place and checked the teller drawers again.

One locked drawer gave way to a sturdy kick by a number twelve boot belonging to Gunner. Inside were more stacks of bills.

They scooped them up, then went through the office and out a door into the bank lobby.

"Right this way, gentlemen," the Professor said. "The back door to the alley is this way. Oh, we did make sure that no one looking in the windows can see anyone tied up, didn't we?"

Gunner shrugged. The Professor ran back toward the front door and pushed the first teller next to the front wall where he couldn't be seen. There were only two windows, and now anyone looking in either one could see that the bank was closed and the workers gone for the day.

The Professor came to the back door. "We go out one at a time and drift down to the general store. Act normally. The bank bags we slip in our saddlebags when nobody is looking. Everybody have some spending money?"

Ten minutes later Willy Boy and Johnny Joe had started stacking up goods they wanted to buy at the general store. They each took two wool blankets at two dollars each, and new western black hats with a low crown on them.

They got canteens, and trail tin dinnerware to serve six, plates, cups, silverware, and some pots and pans.

The store owner, Art Evertson, nodded at them.

" 'Pears you boys going to be taking a trail ride," he said.

" 'Bout the size of it," Willy Boy said. They picked out a sackful of food: a slab of bacon, two loaves of fresh bread, salt, sugar, coffee beans, some cans of sliced peaches, and a bunch of dried fruits and jerky.

When the store owner totaled it up he had a bill of $26. Willy Joe fished in his pocket and came up with a ten and a twenty dollar bill he had put there in advance from the bank loot.

"Why don't I throw in about three gunny sacks or flour sacks you can use to tote that stuff in," Everston said. "Least I can do. Hope you boys have a good trip."

They carried the sacks out of the store and down to their horses. In case the store owner was watching, they tied one sack of goods on each of the two animals, and then led them down the street. They had agreed to meet back at the same camp site they used the night before.

It was a half hour after Willy Boy and Johnny Joe got to the camp before the other three came in. All wore low crowned black hats. The professor had a new shirt and a red checkered vest.

"Took my fancy," the Professor said.

"You each got blankets and canteens and personal gear you wanted?" Willy Boy asked.

"Yeah, sure did," Eagle said. "Almost wouldn't sell me anything until Gunner came up and stared that clerk right into the table."

"We're set," the Professor said. "Where we heading?"

"We know that Sheriff Dunwoody will probably be after us again. We'll watch for him. I've got some business up in Kansas. Figured we might head up that way. Should be able to find out where the Fourteenth Cavalry Regiment is at the same time."

Eagle nodded. He was sharpening his eight-inch hunting knife with a new whetstone he had bought in town.

Gunner nodded. Juan shrugged, Johnny Joe grinned and saluted. The Professor made it unanimous.

"Let's get out of here then before they find out they just lost their bank money," Willy Boy said. "We'll count the cash on our first stop. As I remember, there's a main trail running from the corner of New Mexico across the edge of the Indian Ter-

63

ritories and up to Fort Dodge, Kansas. Shouldn't be hard to find."

"Kansas sounds good," Eagle said. "I haven't been in Kansas yet talking to the army."

"We're not going to wait for Sheriff Dunwoody this time," Willy Boy said. "If he wants us, he'll have to catch us."

They rode hard the rest of the afternoon heading straight north. It was almost dark when they saw a stage coach rattling along a road of sorts. When they got to it they found it was only a trail, but a well used one.

"Must be the trail from Fort Dodge down to some fort in New Mexico," Willy Boy said. "I'd guess we have a ride of about two hundred miles."

The sun was dropping behind the western prairie when they angled to a small stream and found a place to camp behind some cottonwood and a few misplaced live oak trees.

They swung down from their horses and Willy Boy called them around. "Bring your sacks of bank money. Let's count up and divide and see how much we earned for ourselves this afternoon."

"Yeah, yeah," the Professor said.

They dumped the money out on a

blanket and the Professor said he'd had experience counting bank money so they sat back and watched as he did the honors.

"Remember, that was a tiny bank in a small town, so don't expect a hell of a lot."

He counted and dug a small pad of paper and a stub pencil from his pocket and noted down figures as he went along. Then he stacked the double eagle $20 gold coins, and then stacked the smaller gold coins.

When he had it all noted down on the pad he added it. Then he frowned, put down a figure and added the total again. At last he sat back on his heels and looked at them.

"Gentlemen, we took from that little bank $2,466."

"Woweeeeeeeee!" Willy Boy shrilled.

The others yelped in glee and looked back at the Professor.

"That means each of us gets $411. That don't count what we already spent back at that same town."

Juan's eyes went wide. "That's more money than I make in two years!" he said.

"More than I've seen in a long time," Johnny Joe said.

Eagle shook his head. "I never have owned that much real money."

"Divide it up," Willy Boy said. "We won't have a banker, don't want nobody getting any big ideas. We're a team, we busted out together, and if we don't stick together, Dunwoody or some bounty hunter's gonna cut us to pieces."

"I don't got a purse to carry it," Gunner said.

"Next town we get money belts and pocket books," Willy Joe said. "Until then, stash it in your saddlebags."

Eagle put his money away, then he dug a small fire pit and lined the outside of it with dry rocks from the river bank. He made a fire and took the bag of dry beans the rancher had given them.

"If we put them on to cook tonight, and let them cook all night, it's as good as soaking them overnight and cooking them the next day," Eagle explained. "They'll be ready for breakfast and dinner."

Juan looked around to see who was going to be cook. At last he talked to Willy Boy who nodded and Juan began peeling potatoes and dropping them into a pot of water to boil. He fried slices of bacon and gave Eagle three raw slices to put in with the beans. They cut off steaks and fried them as well and sliced the loaves of bread with Eagle's long knife.

When the potatoes were done, Juan dished them out into the six plates, piled on two slices of bacon each, and then slid in a pound of beefsteak fried to a sizzle and added a slice of bread.

The coffee had been boiling and the men had been drinking it as the dinner was readied. They sat around the fire cross-legged, balancing the tin plates on their laps or on a handy rock.

When the meal was over, Eagle tossed his plate in the air and caught it. "I move we elect Juan our full time cook. Best food I've had since I left the tribe about a hundred years ago."

They all shouted and Juan grinned.

"At home I help my wife cook. She has a bad hand and it's hard for her."

"If you think this was good," Eagle said. "Wait until you taste my beans and bacon for breakfast!"

They all hissed and booed.

He grinned. "What the hell, I'll eat them all myself."

When the dinner was cooked, he pushed the coals around his bean pot so the water would keep boiling gently. He added just enough wood to the blaze to keep the heat about even.

As the others rolled out their blankets,

Eagle used a small folding shovel he had bought at the hardware. He dug a hole twice as big as his bean pot next to the fire. He moved over a shovel full of coals and built a new fire in the second fire pit putting on a lot of wood so it would burn down to coals.

"What the hell you doing, Eagle?" Willy Boy asked.

"Making a bed of coals to keep my feet warm tonight," he said.

When the others crawled into their blankets, Eagle poured more fresh water into the bean pot and sealed on the lid. Then he used a pair of gloves and lowered the bean pot into the hole directly on top of six inches of glowing coals. When the pot was in safely, he shoveled dirt from the hole back into the area around the pot. When he got to the top, he took a folded gunny sack and put it over the top of the pot, then covered the whole thing with a mound of dirt.

Willy Boy watched from his blankets. "So that's how you get it to cook all night without tending the fire," he said.

"Old white eye trick," Eagle said. "I learned it from one of the Brothers at Catholic school in San Antonio."

They let the fire die down, and Willy Boy

lay there with his fingers laced together in back of his head staring through the leaves at the stars.

So far, so good. They had food and equipment and arms and were on their way to Kansas to try to find that bastard Deeds Conover. He'd have the Professor make inquiries with the lawmen in the Kansas towns. Sooner or later one of the sheriffs would know where the bounty hunter was. He wasn't liked by the law, but they respected him. He brought in a lot of postered men.

As he drifted off to sleep, Willy Boy was thinking up new kinds of torture for Deeds Conover. He wanted the man scared shitless, screaming for mercy, and agonizing right up to the last minute of hours and hours of physical torture. Yeah!

Morning came with a gust of wind and sunshine. Clouds were building in the west and moving toward them. With luck they could find a stage station or a small town before the angry clouds turned loose and showered them with hail or a cloudburst.

There was time to dig out the bean pot. They had eaten bacon sandwiches for breakfast and three cups of coffee each along with a chew of dried apricots, but the beans interested them.

Eagle dug off the gunny sack and shook it clean, then washed it out in the creek. He lifted off the top of the bean pot and the smell of the white beans cooked with the bacon won them over.

They lined up to spoon out beans on their plates. Eagle stood back and waited until last. Then he tasted them, nodded, sprinkled some salt on them and had another slice of the bread.

"Damn good!" Johnny Joe screeched. "How you learn to do that? My old mom used to soak beans overnight, then cook them for a day and a half."

"White eye much crazy," Eagle said, going into his dumb Indian pose.

They laughed together, ate half the beans and put the rest in a pot with a lid they could seal and strapped it in with the rest of the food. They'd heat the beans up for dinner.

For the next two days they rode toward Kansas. They never were sure when they went through the edge of Indian Territory or when they came into Kansas. They got soaked twice with summer thunderstorms but missed getting struck by lightning.

The third day they came to a small town

and rode directly to the first saloon. It was early afternoon and Gunner bought five bottles of beer at the bar for a dime each and came back and gave each of the men one.

"Where's yours?" Willy Boy asked Gunner.

"Don't drink," Gunner said. "I go kind of crazy."

He stared at them and they nodded.

After two beers they went outside and Willy Boy talked to the Professor for a minute, then he went across the street to the building with the sign on it that said, "Jesse, Kansas City Marshall."

Five minutes later the Professor came back to the horses shaking his head.

"Sorry, Willy Boy, the marshall here never heard of this Deeds Conover. He said there's the county seat down the line about ten miles and they might know about him."

It was getting on toward supper time and they all trooped into the Jesse Cafe and Bakery and had a real supper. The specialty today was beef stew with six different vegetables and cherry pie.

On the way out they bought three loaves of bread and got back on their horses and rode.

They had been putting in long days, and Willy Boy figured they had covered about 40 miles a day. That meant they should be about halfway there. Their horses were holding up good. Willy Boy wondered if Sheriff Dunwoody was still after them.

"Two more days and we should be at the army post," he told Eagle. "You've looked for this army outfit before?"

"Yes, but they usually won't talk to me. If you or the Professor could talk to the Post Commander, he should know where the Fourteenth is, if it's anywhere in this section of the country. I think he'd have a roster or a list showing where every army is stationed."

"I'll do it. I almost joined the army once. Glad now that I didn't. They would have shot me by now for sure. Don't worry, Eagle, we'll find the bastard outfit that shot down your family. I promise you that."

They rode again. Willy Boy was anxious to talk to the county sheriff where they might know something about bounty hunter Deeds Conover. His trigger finger itched just thinking about that bastard!

# Chapter Six

*Sheriff Jim* Dunwoody was sure he had ridden straight into the horrendous jaws of hell when the rifle fire began in that brushy woods near the creek. When the shotgun blasts came he knew he was in the lowest Hades of them all. He ordered the volunteer posse out of there and they rode like demons for a mile.

Six men had been left dead or dying on the small battlefield. The posse stopped and bound up the wounds of the five men who were hurt. Two had minor wounds from the double-ought buck, another had a rifle bullet in his shoulder and two more with serious wounds to the body from the rifles, but they could still ride.

They came to some cover two miles away from the battle scene and stopped again. Sheriff Dunwoody and five men who were not wounded moved slowly back toward the site of the battle.

"Give them killer outlaws time enough to move out," Dunwoody said. "I ain't about to leave six dead men out here alone

73

and without a proper burial."

When they got to the woods again, the outlaws had moved on, and the sheriff and his men picked up the dead. When they couldn't find the men's horses, they draped them over their own mounts behind the saddles and took them back to the rest of the wounded and grieving posse.

The horses were skitterish carrying another man on their backs that way, but they settled down. It was after dark before the posse got back to town.

Now, three hours later, Jim Dunwoody sat in his office staring at the names of the dead men. What the hell was he going to do now? He wasn't going to let the bastards get away with this. Something had to be done. What? Just what the hell could he do now. Go after them. Sure, how?

He'd been in the war, became a Sergeant of Cavalry before he was discharged. Maybe, just maybe he could take a clue from his military service. He thought about it most of the night, then about four o'clock had an idea and fell to sleep in his chair leaning on his arms on the top of his desk.

At nine the next morning he was organizing it. He went from friend to friend around town. By noon he had signed up five good men. That was all he wanted. Six against six, sounded like good odds. He called them together and explained exactly what they would do.

"All of you men are experienced. You all were in the war. You've been blooded. You've all had a friend or relative killed in the past two days by these damn outlaws. What we're going to do is go out hard and fast. We'll cover sixty to seventy miles a day. We'll eat off the land or at farms or towns. We take very little with us besides one blanket, our rifles and revolvers and ammunition. We'll ride down these killers, and we'll cut them down to a man. We won't be bringing back any prisoners."

He looked around. "That's our job. Anybody want to back out?"

He stared at each man, giving everyone a chance.

"No problem if you want out. Some of us might get hurt out there. I hope not. We'll be careful and the only rule is there are no rules. We'll slaughter the sombitches sleeping in their blankets if we can."

None of the men decided to quit.

They left an hour later after eating a large meal and filling their canteens. They rode out of town quietly. Each man carried a begged, borrowed or just bought Henry repeating rifle. They each had 300 rounds of the .44 rifle ammunition for the long gun and 100 for their six-gun. They were ready, grim and determined.

Deputy Seth Matthews begged to come along, but he was still weak and could hardly stand alone. He had sworn that if they didn't bring the outlaws to heel, he would take up the chase just as soon as he was able.

Dunwoody and his posse left town on a lope, retracing their trail that had brought them home with their deadly burdens. They made an average of six miles to the hour, and left just before ten that morning.

They rode at a lope for twelve hours and stopped once at a farm house where the couple gladly fed them. A half hour later they thanked the couple and left. Not a man complained about the pace or the long hours. They knew exactly the kind of men they were going to be facing. They rode on slowing down only a little at dusk.

They had passed the creek of death and picked up the outlaws' tracks. They headed west, out of state.

"We go where they go," Sheriff Dunwoody said. "We have warrants if we need them, and we cross territorial or state lines as we need to. We get the bastards, period!"

The posse kept going. The trail headed toward the town of Clayton in New Mexico Territory. Dunwoody pushed them along the established trail until ten that night, slowing a little at the darkness.

"Closest town of any size," he said. "I figure they'll need some clothes and weapons, maybe even some camping gear and food if they keep on the trail."

The next morning they rode into Clayton, checked with the sheriff and heard about the bank robbery. They stayed only long enough for a good meal, then they made a mile circle around the town and soon picked up clear prints of six horses heading north at a fast pace.

"My guess is they're heading for the Dodge City to Albuquerque, New Mexico trail," Sheriff Dunwoody said. "Heard this Willy Boy was from up that way." They rode hard at six miles to the hour and hit the main trail, but lost the tracks.

The first town they came to moving northeast along the trail was Jesse, Kansas, and Sheriff Dunwoody talked with the lawman there. The town marshall told them that on the day before a stranger had asked about a certain bounty hunter, which was unusual.

"Asked about Deeds Conover?" Dunwoody asked.

The sheriff said that was the gent, and he described the man who had made the inquiry.

Sheriff Dunwoody drove the men out of Jesse fast and up the line. He knew that Willy Boy was trying to find Conover. Evidently the man had wronged Willy Boy somehow. The outlaws were only a day ahead of them. The man described by the lawman as making the inquiries about Conover had been the Professor.

In Halton, the county seat of Morton county, Sheriff Dunwoody quickly established that the outlaws had stopped there, talked with the sheriff and had eaten at a local cafe. Sheriff Dunwoody pulled his men out of town quickly and charged along the trail that led toward Dodge City.

"I expect them to relax once they get to Dodge," Dunwoody said. "It's big enough they can get lost a little. They have money now from that bank robbery back in Clayton. That's the same method of bank robbing that the Professor has used four or five times, so we're certain they came this way. They're too skitterish to stop at a hotel, though. I checked the one hotel back there in Halton, and nobody who even looked like that bunch had checked in."

The best tracker with the sheriff figured they were about six hours behind the outlaws now. It would be too dark to track them in another two hours.

"We push on toward Dodge and hope we can catch them in a camp. Keep your noses peeled for smokes where there shouldn't be any."

They rode.

A bright moon came out with the darkness, three-quarters full, and it made working down the trail across the grasslands easy. They came to two small creeks and slowly paced along them for a half mile but found no camp.

No smokes showed.

Just after nine o'clock that night their best tracker called softly and they all stopped.

"Smoke," he said quietly and began to move ahead toward a pair of cottonwood trees showing against the skyline. As they came closer a horse in the brush nickered a greeting. The men grabbed their horses' muzzles to prevent any answering call to the other horse.

"Damn," Dunwoody said softly. "A horse is almost as good a watchdog as a dog."

He thought about it for a moment. They hadn't moved since the horse called. "Back," he said and they turned and walked the other way. Two hundred yards off they tied their horses to one picket driven into the ground with silent kicks of a boot.

The men gathered around Sheriff Dunwoody.

"We move up on them quietly in a line. Must be some water over there. Somehow we have to decide if that's the outlaws we want. We can't go around killing just anybody."

"What about if they shoot first?" one of the men asked.

"We still got to be sure. I'll yell at Willy Boy. He's crazy enough to call back."

They moved up then, walking slowly, their rifles ready with a round in the chamber. When they got to where they had been with the horses, they paused. All they could see were the two tall cottonwood trees.

They went forward again, Dunwoody leading the way.

At 50 yards, they could see the brush and hear the gentle murmur of a creek. They knelt down now, watching, waiting. Nothing happened. At 30 yards, Dunwoody motioned them to lay down. He did the same.

"Hello there in the camp. Better give it up, Willy Boy."

There was no response.

"I've got 30 guns out here surrounding your camp," Sheriff Dunwoody called. "Better sound off or I'm gonna open fire, Willy Boy. You, too, Professor. No sense killing all of you right here."

"Try it, bastards!" Willy Boy screeched from the brush.

Someone fired from the trees, then five more guns fired two or three shots each.

"Now!" Sheriff Dunwoody screeched.

His men fired from their prone positions, each man sending four shots into the brush at the winking lights of the gunfire.

Someone in the brush screamed and Sheriff Dunwoody brayed his pleasure.

"Kill the bastards!" he screamed.

After eight shots each, some of the outlaws had to stop and reload.

The sheriff's men kept firing, but at a slower rate. Two stopped and reloaded the Henry's long tube magazine under the rifle barrel. A few fired a shot or two from revolvers.

"Anybody hit?" Dunwoody called softly.

Word came back that one man had a

wound, not serious, he said. In the short break the sheriff's men changed positions, spreading out more, one man running almost to the edge of the brush downstream from the position they figured the outlaws held.

Then six pistol shots came from the brush and the sheriff's men fired again. This time it seemed that several of the outlaws fired at the same winking rifleman. Thirty seconds later that sheriff's man stopped firing. Dunwoody watched that development and quit shooting himself. He rolled toward the man who had been ten yards to one side of him. In the soft moonlight, he saw that the whole top of his man's head had been blown away. Sheriff Dunwoody rolled away, grabbed the dead man's Henry rifle and took it with him.

He blasted all of the rounds from both the weapons into the brush camp, then lay there breathing hard. He reloaded one of the Henrys, then lifted it, jumped to his feet and ran forward into the woods this side of the pinpoints of fire.

Dunwoody made it untouched and began walking slowly through the brush toward the camp. He found what he wanted, their horses. He shot one in the head and saw it go down screaming before gunfire erupted a dozen feet from him.

He felt the impact of the round in his shoulder and bellowed in pain, then dropped and rolled and clawed his way to his feet and charged away through the brush.

Too late, he realized he didn't have the Henry. Better losing it than his life. He plowed back to the spot when he had left the deputies and found only one man still firing.

"Pull back!" he bellowed. "Back to the horses."

As he said it six shots snarled toward him, missing by inches. He crawled away for 20 yards before he got up and ran.

He missed the horses and had to circle back. When he found them there were only three men mounted and waiting for him.

"We lost Ed," one of the men said. "He said it was just a scratch, then he died."

"That's two they killed then," Sheriff Dunwoody growled. "Let's pull back." He thought a moment then changed his mind. "No, we'll ride ahead of them toward Dodge. We'll try to be ready for them tomorrow when they come up the trail."

"Christ, Jim, two more dead? I thought we were going to do this right this time."

The speaker was one of his deputies

from town. He had a right to bitch.

"Anybody else hit? I caught one in the shoulder, but I killed one of their horses. We take all six of our horses or kill two of them. We got to slow them down somehow. One horse short for them will mean one of their mounts has to carry double. That will force them to move slower."

They picked up the spare horses and rode. The track was wider now, easier to follow, showing a lot of wagon traffic. They rode for what Dunwoody figured was two hours, then found a small dry stream bed that had some trees and brush and stopped there for the rest of the night.

One of the men tied up the sheriff's shoulder with some strips off his shirt, then they went to sleep. Morning would come too early as it was without wasting a man standing guard duty for half the night.

Dunwoody couldn't sleep. He was exhausted, tired physically, mentally empty, and all of his nervous energy had been spent during the fire fight. He lay huddled in his blanket, his six-gun in his hand.

Why? Why did they have to kill two good men? Those outlaws, those killers, bank robbers, murderers all. They had killed 15, 16 men by now. When would it end? How would it end? For a minute he wanted to turn around and ride back to Oak Park. He could serve out the rest of his term as sheriff, then move on to some new town. These six outlaws weren't worth getting killed for.

He thought that way just for a minute. Then he firmed his resolve. It was his job to bring them in or kill them. He was going to blow them into pieces before he was done with the outlaws.

That's when he remembered the scream from the camp in the trees. They must have hit one of them, maybe wounded him bad so the outlaws couldn't travel fast. Yeah, maybe. Just maybe. It was the best news he had thought of.

At last, with those more favorable thoughts, Sheriff Jim Dunwoody drifted off to sleep.

# Chapter Seven

That's *it*, they're gone," Willy Boy said staring into the darkness. "I can hear their horses galloping away. Geeeeeeehaw! Didn't we give them a reception! Damnation but that was a fine little go-round!"

"One of us got hit," the Professor said quietly. "Who was it caught a slug?"

"Me," Johnny Joe Williams said from a dozen feet away.

"Get over here and let's take a look," Willy Boy said. "Juan, come take a look at this."

They shielded the light with their bodies and Eagle lit a torch he had whittled with a lot of fringe edges on it so it flamed up brightly.

Johnny Joe looked pale in the harsh fire light. The slug had caught him high in the chest. Juan pulled open his shirt and looked at the entry wound.

"Should be above your lung," Juan said. "You having any trouble getting your breath?"

Johnny Joe winced as he shook his head.

"Good. Let's look at your back." He hoisted up Johnny Joe's shirt and Eagle moved the torch to that side. There was an inch wide bloody wound running a stream of blood. Juan took a clean handkerchief and pressed on the wound.

"Neckerchiefs," he said, and the men pulled them off and gave them to him. He folded one and put it on the front wound and had the Professor hold both in place. Then he tied the other neckerchiefs together and wrapped them around Johnny Joe's chest wound and his back and under his arm.

"Not the best bandage, but we'll make it do until morning. You shouldn't be riding anywhere tomorrow. Maybe we should move to a better defensive spot and lay over for a day or two."

"We lost a horse," Eagle said. "One of them slipped into the brush and shot one of the mounts in the head. She went down and dead in a minute. I hit the guy with a pistol shot but he kept on running."

"So, we take stock in the morning. Eagle, can you stand guard for the rest of the night? Don't want them bastards slipping up on us again."

"Yes, I'll be on guard," Eagle said. "They rode out to the north. Might be planning on bushwhacking us tomorrow as we ride by."

"We might not ride by," Willy Boy said. "We got no timetable, excepting to get Johnny Joe fixed up." His face frowned in the light of the torch. "Where the hell did they come from, that town where we robbed the bank?"

"Not a chance," the Professor said. "He knew your name. Got to be the sheriff from Oak Park, our friend Dunwoody. He's a hard man to shake."

"Maybe we should shake him for good tomorrow. How many were there?"

"Six," Eagle said. "But now four or five. One of them got put out for good in that fire fight. I don't think they took their dead with them. I'll go out and check for sure." He handed the torch to Willy Boy who put it out on the ground.

"Yeah, check them. If they're shot up, they might be heading home. If not, we should make sure they don't bother us again. We can always kill the ones left."

"Remember, we're short a horse," Gunner said. "Maybe they left one."

"Eagle will know," Willy Boy said. "Now, let's get to sleep. Do the best you can, Johnny Joe. We'll figure out tomorrow how to patch you up. We can't backtrack. If that is the Oak Park sheriff, he left word about us on our back trail."

"Sure they aren't coming back?" Johnny Joe asked.

"Damn certain, now try to get some sleep." Willy Boy watched the wounded man lay on his side, then turn on his back and then to his side again.

Willy Boy watched the rest of the camp settle down. He thought about Johnny Joe and snorted. What was this? Why was he worried about the kid? A month ago he would have ridden off without a word. Now, somehow, the kid made a difference. Yeah, the guy had helped them break out. They had fought together. He was one of the six, The Outlaws, one of a group.

And Willy Boy was the group's leader.

So, he had a gang. So he had to think about each of the members or they wouldn't be in his bunch. The group gave them all safety, he'd told them that. Damn, now he was starting to believe it himself.

Either one of the posses could have run down one or two men and killed or captured them. With six it became a goddamned war. Most of these posses didn't like to fight a war.

Hell, right now it was ride tall or hang high.

They had to stick together, which meant they had to take care of Johnny Joe. Next town they'd find a doctor, make him fix up Johnny Joe, or else. Yeah. Next town.

Eagle came back, running into camp with that Indian trot he had learned as a kid with the Comanches. He came directly to Willy Boy.

"We killed two of them. Two out of six. Can't figure out why they left their dead out there."

"They was getting their asses shot off is why. Probably plan on coming back for them later."

"Maybe," the black eyes of the Indian glittered in the moonlight. "I went over to where I could smell their horses. None left there, so they took all six. We need another horse."

"We'll get one at the next ranch we pass. We can buy one, we got money. Horse and saddle. Right now we don't need nobody else gunning for us."

"Johnny Joe?"

"Damn right, we take care of Johnny Joe. What the hell's wrong with that, you redskin savage?"

"Nothing, white eye."

Suddenly they were both grinning.

"Think we hurt any of the others?" Willy Boy asked.

"I'll look for dried blood in the morning," Eagle said. "Know I winged one by our dead horse. I'll check the other firing positions. They were using Henrys so there'll be some brass out there."

"Get some sleep."

"No guard?"

"Hell, no. The last four in that posse are scared so bad they're about to piss their pants. Get us up at dawn."

With dawn, Willy Boy came awake slowly. Eagle had been up for ten minutes, found a lot of blood where the dead horse lay and on a drip line out to the firing positions. There he found what could have been where another wounded man bled. He had checked around as far as he could see and couldn't find a stray horse.

They left that morning without a fire or breakfast. They had no idea how far the next town was. They rode down the trail for half an hour, then went off the track to the right by half a mile and rode just so they could see the scar across the edge of the grasslands. They saw a ranch to the left, but it was three or four miles, and they didn't want to make that long a detour.

They passed several clumps of trees and brushy creeks, but kept well off the trail so any bushwhacking attempt by the sheriff could not take place. Just before ten that morning, they saw a small town coming up.

They had made the trip with Johnny Joe riding double behind Willy Boy, since he was the lightest of the group and the double riders would not be that much harder on the horse.

The Professor checked with Willy Boy, then rode faster into town to see if a strange posse had been there and to find where the doctor's office was.

Eagle met them at the edge of town and they circled around Main Street to the other side of the village to a white painted house and attached office. The doctor was in.

The medical man had only one other patient and when he saw the chest wound he hurried Johnny Joe straight through into a small room and lay him down on a high table. He probed a moment, looked at the wound in back and completed the removal of the makeshift bandages.

The doctor was small, thin, about 60 and bounced around like a rubber ball.

"Mmmm. By rights you should be half dead, son. That there slug missed the top of your lung by a quarter-of-an-inch, I'd say. Ever have a hole in your lung? Whole damn thing can collapse and you might take your last breath in a rush. Sure, some folks live with one lung, but not the best kind of life.

"Near as I can tell, that chunk of lead didn't do much else in the way of damage. Most likely cracked a rib going in and maybe another one coming out. Pain'll be terrible for a week or two, but you'll heal. You're young."

He washed off the puncture wound with some kind of watery looking substance, then put salve and ointment on the wound. He did the same thing on the back one, then bandaged them both with sticky tape to hold the compresses in place.

"Bed rest for at least a week. No running around, and damn sure no horseback riding. Hear me, son?"

Johnny Joe nodded.

Willy Boy and the Professor had helped Johnny Joe walk into the office and waited during the doctoring. Now Willy Boy asked the sawbones about his fee and he looked up quickly.

"Mean you can pay in real money? No chickens or spuds or maybe a quarter of a steer? By crackies, hardly know what to say. Two dollars'll be fine."

Willy Boy gave him a two dollar gold

piece and the doctor handed him a small jar of the salve. "Put some of that on the wounds each time you change the bandages."

The sawbones looked at them, then dug into a drawer and took out half a dozen of the square compresses, some thin rolls of bandage and a roll of the white sticky tape. He handed them to Willy Boy, who gave him another dollar bill.

Outside they got a report from Juan and Eagle. Nobody had seen four riders come into town.

They had a big meal at a cafe and as they finished, the Professor checked in with the local law, but they didn't know anything about a bounty hunter named Deeds Conover.

Johnny Joe wheezed softly as he breathed, and held one shoulder lower than the other.

"Don't hurt quite so damn much that way," he explained.

They finished their second cup of coffee and looked at each other. At last Willy Boy asked the question.

"Johnny Joe, you feel like riding on toward Dodge? Not sure how far it is now, two days at least."

"Hurt worst last night, better today. I can make it if we walk the horses. Would like to have one to myself, though."

They bought a horse and saddle at the livery stable and rode out of town. They were a mile past sight of the town, where the trail northeast went through a small creek, that it happened.

With proper discipline of his men, Sheriff Dunwoody could have killed all six of the outlaws.

The outlaws rode into the small ford through the brushy woods as a bunched group, two ahead, three abreast and Eagle bringing up the rear. One of the four men left in Dunwoody's crew fired too soon. Willy Boy and his gang had just started into the brush which was about 30 yards wide at the roadway.

The first Henry rifle round slammed into Willy Boy's saddle an inch from his leg and he kicked his horse in the flanks and drove it into the brush moving away from the side where the gunshot sounded.

The shot warned the other five. Johnny Joe, who rode just behind Willy Boy, kicked his mount and lay against the animal's neck and galloped straight ahead and out of the line of fire and to safety.

The three in the center — the Professor, Juan and Gunner — rode in three directions. Gunner rode to the left straight at the man who had fired. The Professor and Juan swung to the right and galloped into the brush and trees away from the line of fire.

Behind them, Eagle heard the shot, jerked his mount around and rode back the way they had come for 50 yards, then swinging off the saddle to the right until he was hidden behind the horse, holding on only by his left stirrup and a handful of mane, he angled the horse into the protective cover of the brush and trees.

Willy Boy broke into the brush, kicked out of the saddle, dropped to the ground and dove behind a cottonwood. He stood and looked where the pall of blue smoke settled around a tree across the trail. He lifted his Spencer, aimed at the tree and waited.

A form stood up near the tree and looked around it. Willy Boy tightened his finger on the trigger as he realigned his sights and fired. He saw the man's head explode into a gush of red froth as the bullet slammed through his skull.

Willy Boy dropped to the ground out of sight while the blue cloud of smoke gave away his position.

Gunner had charged into the brush, saw a man bring up a rifle and Gunner shot him with his pistol before the man could sight in the long gun. Gunner kept riding directly past the downed posse man, then swung wide through the brush and back to the road as he raced after Johnny Joe who was now a quarter-of-a-mile down the trail.

Juan and the Professor had dropped off their horses as well, aware that they were massive targets while mounted. They lay in the brush, flat on the ground, listening.

Juan pointed to the left. They both looked that way but saw nothing. A minute later they heard the familiar sound of a Spencer firing with its .52 caliber voice. They had heard Gunner's six-gun go off a half a minute earlier. Now they lay there silently and waited.

Soon they heard low voices across the trail, then the sound of someone running. A few seconds later horses' hooves pounded on the ground and they had a fleeting glance as two horses burst from the trees and raced back down the road, south. They galloped flat out.

By the time Juan and the Professor got to the trail, the horsemen were out of effective range. Then another horse came out of the brush to chase them. They saw Eagle riding and as he came up quickly on the two riders, he slipped off his saddle to the right. He swung his mount around to the pair of sheriff's possemen, bent under his horse's neck and fired his six-gun.

The confused pair of men had no target. They looked in surprise at the riderless horse slamming along beside them. Then the revolver sounded four times, and the nearest man tumbled off his horse onto the ground.

Eagle swung back up in the saddle, turned his mount and walked back to where the posse rider lay sprawled on the trail. He would ride no more. Eagle dropped out of his saddle, picked up the dead man's Henry repeating rifle and his six-gun, remounted and rode back for the ford across the small creek. He paused, then rode on north.

The outlaws gathered a half mile beyond the ambush. Johnny Joe sat his horse shaking his head.

"Stupid fool luck," he said. "We all should be dead right now. Hell, if we'd set up that ambush it would have worked."

"Somebody fired before he should have," Willy Boy said. "He not only fired too quick, the damned fool also missed. He should have blown me out of the saddle. Led me a little too much."

"It was the sheriff who got away," Eagle said. "I had to take the man who was nearest me, and by then the sheriff was out of range."

"Five out of six ain't bad," Johnny Joe said.

Gunner nodded. "They shouldn't have tried to bushwhack us that way. They were not nice men."

"Can't fault you on that, Gunner," the Professor said. He looked at Johnny Joe. "How's the bandages? You making it?"

"So far, but I sure as hell could use a bed to sleep in tonight."

Willy Boy nodded. "Now that seems like a good idea. I'd almost bet my last peso that our friend Sheriff Dunwoody doesn't come pestering us anymore. Let's get down to the next town, go in twos, and register at the best hotel in town. Everyone still have some cash money?"

They all did.

"Fine, let's ride. We're still a day and a half away from Dodge."

# Chapter Eight

As *the* six men rode along the trail toward Dodge, Willy Boy kept thinking about Deeds Conover and that terrible night when the man had killed his father, then tried for the son with one more round from the double barreled shotgun.

Willy Boy had jumped through a window as the bounty man grabbed at his revolver and took four more shots at Willy Boy as he ran screaming and bleeding into the night.

He had darted through the blackness simply running for his life. It was pure luck that he was alive. He was only 14, so he had run into the fields and got lost in the tall corn and the darkness.

When he heard the man ride away, Willy Boy slipped back to the house and found his pa's big six-gun and figured out how to load it. Then he shortened the belt so he could hold it up on his slender hips, and strapped it on.

He hadn't dared to stay there in the house that night. But it was a warm late

July evening, so he took two good wool blankets, saddled up his horse and as a last thought, grabbed a rifle and some shells. Before he left, he found the tobacco tin where his pa kept his cash money.

Small farmers didn't ever have much money, Willy Boy knew that. In the thin flat tin, he found $13 and some change. He was rich! He packed what traveling food he could find in the kitchen and headed for Texas. He had an uncle there he knew and liked. Maybe he could work on his small ranch.

He rode then, fearful that the bounty hunter killer would come back. That first night he slept cold and miserable under some brush a mile from the house.

By the next afternoon when he slipped into the country store at the crossroads, he heard about the bounty hunter in the area looking for a wanted man.

"Blamed fool shot the wrong man," the store owner, Mr. Jacobs, told a customer as he weighed out a pound of eight penny box nails. "Gunned down Hartley Lambier with a shotgun. Then he took off like hell was hounding him before the sheriff could even get out to the place. Won't see nothing of Deeds Conover around here for a long spell."

The name burned into Willy Boy's consciousness. Deeds Conover, Deeds Conover, Deeds Conover. He would never forget the name or the look of the long lanky Texas cowboy, the bounty hunter.

That first day Willy Boy turned west hoping Texas was in that direction. Willy Boy wasn't sure that was right and was too afraid of everyone to ask directions, since he knew he looked like a kid. He was short even for fourteen, and hadn't shaved yet, but he'd had to make do most of his life because his Ma died so far back he couldn't even remember what she looked like.

The first few days he rode and camped out. That's when he realized he didn't even have matches. He bought some at a country store and some bread and peanut butter.

The fourth day he met another kid riding in the same direction. He was about Willy Boy's age. They camped together and shared their food. The next morning the other boy was gone, with Willy Boy's tobacco can of money and his father's rifle. The only reason he didn't take his six-gun was because it was in Willy Boy's hand.

A day later he was hungry and mad at everyone, especially the kid who stole from him. He knew about saloons. From time to time he had helped his father home from one. Now he rode to the next small town, found a saloon and went up the alley behind it. The third man who came out to go to the outhouse teetered and could barely walk.

Willy Boy helped him, and as he did slipped his hand in the man's pockets and pulled out his purse and a gold watch. When the drunk came out of the outhouse, Willy Boy was a mile out of town riding for the next place where he could sell the watch. The purse had only four dollars in it, but the watch was gold filled and worth at least ten dollars.

He got five for it, and whenever he ran out of money, he rolled drunks behind saloons.

Three days later he arrived in Kansas City. He'd never been to such a big town before. He stayed in a hotel for the first time in his life, paid fifty cents for a room all his own, and left his horse on the street.

The next morning his horse, saddle and two blankets were all gone, stolen.

He thought of going to the sheriff, but he didn't know where to find one. He stood on the street almost ready to cry, but refusing to because he was 14.

A man came by and stopped and looked at him.

"Some trouble you're in, boy?" the man asked. He was tall, wore a dark blue suit and a derby hat. He had a fancy tie around his neck and a shirt with a ruffled front.

Willy told him about his horse and gear.

"Well, now, that's not very neighborly of us big city folks, is it? Where do you live?"

"In Missouri."

"Kansas City is in Missouri." The man smiled. "Would you like to have an early supper? Why don't we go into this cafe and have something to eat. I bet you're hungry. Looks like you could use some good food."

"I don't take charity." Willy Boy had heard his dad say that a lot of times.

"Sir, this isn't charity, it's one friend doing a good deed for another friend."

They had beef stew with carrots, peas, turnips, potatoes, parsnips and big chunks of good beef, slices of sweet bread and all the milk he could drink. When they finished they walked out to the street.

The man in the dark blue suit and derby hat smiled. "You know, I have a jacket that would just about fit you. I have no use of it and I'll sell it to you for a dime. Do you have a ten cent piece?"

Willy Boy nodded. The last drunk he

had helped to the outhouse had a twenty dollar gold piece and three singles in his pocket. Willy Boy still had them.

"Tell you what, let's go into the hotel and you can look at the jacket, I'm on the fourth floor front."

They climbed the stairs and then went to the man's room. He took off his suit coat and said he needed a small drink after the long climb. He offered Willy Boy a sarsaparilla. He knew that was a drink for kids, so he took it.

He drank about half of it and then felt woozy and then sleepy. He tried to stay awake by opening his eyes wide, but fell on the bed and slept at once.

When Willy Boy woke up, the man was gone. His clothes were on the chair so maybe the man was taking a bath in the room down the hall. Hell, this was easier than rolling drunks. He'd best move fast before the man returned.

Willy Boy felt to see that his gold piece was still in his pocket. Then he picked up the man's suit pants and took out his wallet. He dumped out the change, two gold coins, five or six bills and stuffed them in his pocket.

Willy Boy quickly left the room. He took the door key that was inside hanging out of the lock. On the outside he locked the door, and threw the key down the hall.

Back on the street he walked all the way to the other side of town and rented a hotel room. This one cost him a dollar. He had taken almost $30 from the tall, blue-suited man. It had been easy.

Now he had to buy a horse and a saddle and a bridle. He'd need more money. That night Willy Boy worked a row of saloons. He helped eight men to the outhouse and picked the purses from all eight.

Back in his hotel room he sorted out the change and bills and gold coins. None of the men had much. From the eight he totaled $43.85. Not a fortune, but enough for a horse and saddle. He would stay there one more day, buy a new jacket and a cowboy hat and another pair of pants. Then he'd work the next street of saloons, and the day after that he'd buy a horse and head on for Texas.

The bed was soft, his door was locked and a chair stood in front of it so he could tell if anyone tried to get in. He slept better than he had in a week.

The next day, just as it got dark, Willy Boy put on his old hat and jacket and found another promising string of saloons. He was working his third drunk when the man felt his pickpocketing and whirled, reaching for his gun.

"Little devil, what you doing, trying to rob me? I ain't that drunk, boy. We better take you to the sheriff."

He had drawn his revolver by then but Willy Boy pulled out the big .44 and shot the man at point blank range before the other weapon came up. The round bored through the man's heart.

Willy Boy started to turn when a big fist slammed down on his gunhand, jolting the weapon from his fingers. Strong arms banded round his chest pinning his arms to his sides.

"Damn, I think we got a killer here," the man said.

The shot had brought a dozen men into the alley.

"Somebody go get the sheriff, damn quick!" another voice said. "This kid just killed Harry Limpton, the mayor's cousin!"

Two days later the trial was held. A witness had seen it all. He had come out of the saloon just behind Limpton, saw Willy Boy offer to help and the whole thing.

Willy Boy had a local lawyer. The barrister discovered that when Willy Boy was arrested he had $72.83 on his person that the sheriff was holding for him. The lawyer agreed to defend Willy Boy for $72.00.

The trial lasted almost an hour. Willy Boy was convicted by a jury of twelve men. They deliberated in the jury box for about five minutes, then gave the judge the unanimous verdict.

Willy Boy was sentenced to hang three days hence along with two other killers.

The second night he was in jail he called the guard. His face was blue, he couldn't breathe. A doctor came quickly and the second the cell door opened, Willy Boy exploded into action grabbing the deputy's gun. They struggled and he killed the deputy. Without a wasted motion, Willy Boy locked the doctor in his cell. Then he found his six-gun in the office, took a rifle from the gun rack and walked out of the jail's back door.

The other two murderers pleaded with him to let them out. He threw them the keys and walked out to the alley. There he stole the deputy's own horse and rode out of Kansas City as fast as he could. He rode the horse until it went lame. Then he walked to the nearest town, stole another horse and rode again. Now he knew Texas was to the south. That was where he was headed.

For the next year, Willy Boy worked south into Texas. At every county seat he had a talk with the sheriff. He was hunting for his father who was a bounty hunter named Deeds Conover. Some of the sheriffs had heard of the man. Most who had, didn't like him, but no one knew where he was right then. He hadn't been through that area lately.

Willy Boy kept looking. He moved up from drunks and began to rob general stores. He'd hit the store just at closing time. Lock the front door for the friendly store owner, then buy some shells for his cartridge revolver and promptly hold up the merchant. He'd tie him up and clean out the cash drawer and maybe take a new gun if he fancied one.

By the time the store owner was found, often late at night by a family member or the next morning by a clerk, Willy Boy was halfway to the next town.

Willy Boy quickly learned that Fridays and Saturdays were the biggest sales days for the stores, and the best time to rob them. His best haul from a general store was $212. With a clerk earning $35 a month and a cowboy $25 a month, $200 was a lot of cash money. He bought a new horse that time, a beautiful deep reddish sorrel with a nearly white mane and tail.

His next real trouble came in southern

Texas. He heard about Deeds Conover. He had brought in a man to a sheriff near Austin. The sheriff was out of town and had to sign the arrest form and verify that the capture had been made, even though the prisoner had died while trying to escape.

Willy Boy found out that Deeds Conover was staying at the Roundup Hotel in Austin. When he got there, Conover had checked out. He almost caught him on the trail out to the town of Fairbanks.

Willy Boy didn't know if Conover knew someone was tracking him, but he slipped in and out of the sheriff's office in Fairbanks in ten minutes while Willy Boy was having his dinner. That night Willy Boy had too many beers in a saloon to drown his disappointment. He had never drank much before and he went a little crazy.

Somebody pushed him and he pushed back, the next thing they knew the two men reached for guns. The other man's weapon hung up in the holster and he couldn't get it out. Willy Boy shot him in the chest and ran out the door and rode out of town before anyone could stop him.

He'd been running ever since.

There were some posters out on him by now. One in Texas that he knew about, but he doubted anywhere else. He kept on the trail of Deeds Conover, crossed his tracks three times. Then Conover went to Oak Park, Texas, to grab a wanted bank robber for a $500 payoff.

This time Willy Boy saw the bastard. Saw him walking down the street while Willy Boy was eating in a cafe. By the time he got out to the Oak Park street the man was gone, and Willy Boy never found him. He got drunk again, shot down someone who objected to his behavior and this time got slugged from behind before he could get away.

Now he was on the trail of the bounty hunter again, this time with five guns to back him up. Five guns and five men who were growing more loyal and more bound together every day.

# Chapter Nine

The six oulaws rode into Dodge in mid-afternoon, had a beer to clean the trail dust out of their throats, then took hotel rooms. They registered in pairs, with rooms next to each other. No sense setting up a six-man party in town.

From there they went separate ways.

The Professor ordered up a bath and bought two new sets of clothes.

Juan bought a new pair of jeans and a shirt and four pairs of socks.

Gunner made sure that Willy Boy was settled in, then lay down on the bed and took a nap.

Johnny Joe went to see a doctor, who changed the dressings and said the healing process had begun. He guessed that the bullet had come close to the lung but did no damage. He did wonder if one of the cracked ribs had bent in and created a small hole in the lung.

"We'd call that a pneumothorax, if it happened. That's when some air gets out of the lung between the rib cage and the lung and can cause all sorts of problems." He grinned. "Don't look like that happened to you or you wouldn't be breathing so well. You're on the healing side of things now. Just try not to break open that healing in the back."

Eagle lay on his bed and read a stack of dime novels about the wild west. He guffawed regularly as he read, wondering how anyone could make up such wild stories about either the Indians or gunfighters.

Willy Boy was going to check with the sheriff about the bounty hunter, but the Professor persuaded him it would be better if he went.

The Professor came back a half hour later. He said quickly that no word had been heard of the bounty hunter.

"Then I got to look through his wanted posters. Told him I was a part time bounty hunter myself and wondered what he had that was new. He gave me a stack half a foot high and I started going through them. Fourth one down from the top was this one."

WANTED . . . DEAD OR ALIVE . . .
THE WILLY BOY GANG
Willy Boy Lambier and five members
of his gang broke out of the Oak Park,

Texas, jail killing two deputies. They later killed 11 members of two posses chasing them.

They are thought to be headed north from Texas. Others in the party include Juan Romero, Nathan Thadius (The Professor), Johnny Joe Williams, Gunner Johnson, and Brave Eagle (a Comanche Indian).

A REWARD OF $2,000 IS OFFERED FOR EACH OF THE ABOVE.

Contact Sheriff Jim Dunwoody, Oak Park, Texas.

Willie Boy put down the wanted poster and grinned. "Hey, that's more reward than the last poster I saw offered for Billy the Kid!"

Willy looked at it again. "Damn good thing they don't have any pictures on this thing." He chuckled. "Nathan Thadius?" he asked looking at the Professor. "Good Lord in a hand bucket, no wonder you changed your name."

"Almost as bad as Lambier. If I hear you use my real name again, young William Lambier, I'll slit your throat ear to ear!"

Willy Boy laughed, but wasn't sure just how much of that threat had been real. He never used the Professor's real name again.

"We got to tell the others about this," Willy Boy said. "I'll show it to them, but I won't let them read your name," he said to the Professor. "Somebody else could go through that stack of Wanteds. Oh, yeah, we got the poster now, the sheriff don't. Would they send out two of them?"

"Doubt it. Anyway, I'm not letting that stop me from getting a store bought shave and a hair wash and hair cut." He looked at Willy Boy. "You could stand a trim as well."

"Not me. Longer hair makes me feel stronger, like Samson. Remember that?"

"Remember ain't believing," the Professor said and went back down to the street to get his haircut.

Willy Boy walked the town. It was smaller than he figured from all the stories he had heard about it. He wasn't even sure who the sheriff was now. From time to time they had had famous gunfighters as sheriff here in Dodge.

He checked a clock in a jeweler's window. Still time enough to ride out to Fort Dodge and see what he could find out for Eagle. He went back to his mount and took a ride. The fort was less than a mile from town.

After talking to a sentry, a Guard Lieu-

115

tenant and then a First Sergeant, he at last got to see the Fort Adjutant, a Lieutenant Parson.

Quickly he outlined what he was trying to discover.

"See, Lieutenant. I got a brother with that outfit, the Fourteenth Cavalry Regiment, and I sure would like to know where he's stationed."

"Can't say for sure, but last I knew of it, the Fourteenth was up at Fort Boise in Idaho. Long way from here."

"You positive they're up there, Lieutenant?"

"That's what my latest roster of assignments shows. I'm not supposed to be telling you this, so if anybody asks me, I never even heard of you." He grinned.

"Yeah, all right. Thanks, Lieutenant. Might be a few days before I get up that direction."

Willy Boy rode back to Dodge wondering how to tell Eagle, or if he should tell him. If Eagle knew where they were, he might ride up there and get himself killed. He'd think on it. First came Deeds Conover. Where should he look to find that bastard?

They had supper that night at the hotel dining room. It wasn't as fancy as some and they sat at different tables, two by two. He had warned them all when he showed them the wanted poster that they would do nothing publicly as a group.

"Don't want somebody getting curious about where that wanted poster went to if anybody makes the connection. Probably not more than two or three deputies saw it, but no sense in taking chances."

They had decided to relax for a few days in Dodge. Nothing special, no worries, just have some fun, spend some money, but not too much, and rest up.

That night Johnny Joe felt good enough to pay a visit to one of the gambling emporiums. He took a beer to a table and slid into a vacant seat. He had $50 worth of chips and the three other players around the table grinned.

"Fresh money," one man said who wore a suit and could be a banker. A cowhand across from him belched, drank half of a mug of beer and pointed at the banker type. "Shut up and deal," he said.

The third man was a towner, in shirt sleeves held up with garters and a green eyeshade. Johnny Joe discounted the other two but watched as the black suit dealt.

It was five card stud and it was a no limit game with table stakes. Johnny Joe lost the first three hands, investing $12 total. His old granddaddy taught him to play the game and ordered him never to win the first hand no matter how good a hand he had.

He won the fourth hand, a seven card stud game and took in a pot worth over $30. He kept working, dumping when he was out of it, playing it smart and never bluffing. By the end of two hours he was about $50 ahead.

The other two men bowed out and Johnny Joe was left with the man with the green eyeshade and the runny, weak blue eyes.

"Cut for high card for $100?" the green eyeshade asked.

Johnny Joe laughed politely. "Do I really look that stupid? That's a sucker bet, especially with a used deck of cards. Would you offer the same thing with a new deck with an unbroken seal and I get to shuffle and cut?"

The green eyeshade took his turn chuckling. "Not a chance. How about showdown at $10 a hand?"

"You know we're talking the pure luck of the draw here, no skill involved, no betting," Johnny Joe said.

"True. My luck has been good tonight. I'll make a side bet of $50 that I win more of the ten hands than you do."

Johnny Joe looked at the man. He was no country bumpkin. He was sure he hadn't seen the man before or played with him, but he knew the routine.

Slowly Johnny shook his head. "I'm a gambler, not a fool. I only bet on a hand that has a chance of winning. I'm more willing to bet on a sure thing. I don't play along with your Mississippi River Boat gambling game. How long has it been since you've worked the boats?"

The man looked up and nodded. "Thought you knew your way around. A cautious, by the odds player. You'll win more times than you lose. What are you ahead right now?"

"About $50."

"Two months wages for a cowhand out there on the range in the dust and wind and rain and sleet." The man grinned. "I know, I started out as a cowhand, before I figured out a better and damn lot easier way to make a living."

Johnny Joe signalled for a pair of frosty beers and looked up at the man. "You ever cheat when gambling?"

The green eyeshade man smiled. "Only when I catch someone cheating against me. I love to watch a cheater know he has say, aces over queens, and I beat him with four deuces."

They both chuckled.

"You staying around long?" the green eyeshade man asked.

"Maybe a week or so."

"Make you a deal. You see me in a game, find another table. If I find you playing, I'll go to another saloon or another table. No sense a couple of professionals beating each other to death."

They lifted the new beers and sealed the agreement, then Johnny Joe started feeling the weariness that had been his constant companion ever since he took that rifle bullet through his chest. He tipped his hat, stifled a groan, and walked over and cashed in his chips. Then he went directly back to his hotel room.

Nobody bothered him. He locked his door and eased down on the bed. The only way he could sleep with any comfort was on his side. He settled down and slept.

The Professor came to Willy Boy's room about eight that night with a bottle of whiskey in one hand and two glasses in the other.

"Busy?" he asked.

Willy Boy waved him inside.

The Professor poured both glasses half full of the amber fluid and handed one to Willy Boy.

"Got a good long look at the bank in town this afternoon just before it closed. I changed a five dollar bill. Place is built like a whole damn vault. One door in and out. Armed guard beside the door. Both tellers have loaded revolvers showing at their cages. The manager has a sawed off shotgun in a quick grab clamp right behind his desk. I saw alarm signals of some kind, chain pulls I think they were.

"The teller pulls a chain or a rope and that sets a spring loaded bell of some kind ringing until it's wound down. The place is impossible. Glad we aren't going to try to rob that one."

"Who says we aren't going to take out that bank?" Willy Boy asked.

The Professor almost swallowed the whiskey glass. He recovered and looked at Willy Boy and saw him laughing.

"Don't scare me that way. I'm depressed enough as it is about the security at that bank."

"There you go, using big words again. Somebody told me you went to college?"

"That is entirely true, young man. I matriculated at Illinois College in Jacksonville, Illinois, for a year and a half. From that endeavor I went on to teach grades one through twelve in Swan Lake, Illinois, for two entire school years from 1866 to '68. After that was over, I resigned and came West."

"What was the first bank that you robbed?"

"You are full of questions, aren't you." He watched Willy Boy for a minute. "Should have brought you a beer, forgot you're not much of a whiskey drinker. You'll learn."

"Yeah, if I live long enough. Hell, I don't plan on living much over 25."

"Don't say that, I'm 24 already. Let's see, first bank I took over. That's easy. It was with Wild Bill Cranston. We got liquored up one night and went into the local bank at some little town in Kansas. I forget the name. We dropped in through the skylight. Then we busted open the old safe they had with a crowbar and a sledge hammer we brought along and went out the back door with over $600."

The Professor broke up laughing. "Wasn't until the next day, when the president of the bank reported his loss, that he said the damn fool robbers had missed over $3,000 in a drawer below the one we had opened!"

The Professor emptied his glass and looked at Willy Boy. "So you see, I was not the smartest of bank robbers when I began. But I learned fast."

"Now you know which banks not to try to rob?"

"Damn betcha!"

"Sounds like a good way to live to be more than 25, if anybody would want to."

"You how old, Willy Boy?"

"Seventeen. Seventeen and nearly a half. Been on my own since I was fourteen."

"Good for you. Now what the hell we gonna do next? Where we going? I can't do any bank robbing in Dodge."

"I'm still looking for the bounty hunter who killed my Pa. He's got to be here somewhere. One of the sheriffs said he thought he worked mostly in Kansas."

"What happens if you find him?"

Willy Boy lay back on the bed, his hands behind his head. He looked at the ceiling. "Nothing quick. I'm gonna capture the bastard, then learn all the torture tricks the Comanches use from Eagle. After that, Deeds Conover is going to die as slowly as possible with as much pain as he can stand without passing out. I think to finish him off I'll hang him head down over a fire and watch his brains fry and his skull explode."

"Willy Boy, you got some wild ideas. Until we find him, we need something to do. We gonna do some more banks, I hope."

"Yeah, why not. Just so we don't get too damn many posses chasing us. My first job is to find that murdering bounty hunter Deeds Conover."

"We'll find him, Willy. Don't worry. We'll find him. And now we're six to one, not him trying to gun down some unarmed 14 year old."

Willy Boy went to the window and lifted it fully open and stuck his head outside.

"Deeds Conover, you murdering bastard! Where the hell are you hiding?"

Willy Boy pulled his head back in and grinned. "If he's in town, that just might rattle him out of his hole."

# Chapter Ten

The *morning* after Willy Boy and his gang arrived in town, a man thumbed through the stack of wanted posters in the sheriff's office in Dodge.

"It's not here," Lars Swenson said looking up at his boss, Michael Handshoe. Swenson was small, reedy, with a thin face and a struggling moustache in gray and black. His watery eyes held a note of panic.

"Damn, it's not here," Lars said again. "We saw it yesterday, five or six down in the stack like it came in recently."

Michael Handshoe was the opposite of Lars. He stretched up to six-feet-two inches, and had a bull like body to match the tallness. One ham like hand pushed Lars aside and fingers worked through the stack of wanted posters on the sheriff's desk.

He went all the way through the pile of over a hundred wanted posters from all over the western United States and territories. When he finished he growled.

"Goddamn, you're right. It was here

before and it ain't now. What the hell kind of sheriff we got here in Dodge anyway?"

"A damn good one," Sheriff Manson said walking into his office. "What the hell kind of bounty hunters we got running around Dodge?"

"Damn good ones, Manson," Handshoe said, holding out his big palm for a shake. "We got a small problem, Sheriff. We saw a wanted poster here yesterday, and today we can't find it. You throw out a batch or something?"

"Ain't likely. People go through the stack beside you boys. Fact is, I've known you to *borrow* a Wanted or two so no other bounty man would look for the gents. I figure it could have happened again."

"Yeah, could. I'm interested in this Willy Boy Gang. Know anything about them?"

"Just what it said on the flyer. What was it, five or six of them, all broke out of jail at the same time down in Texas as I recall. Pay seemed a mite high."

"What I remembered," Handshoe said. "Two thousand each, that makes twelve thousand dollars. A mite tidy sum."

"Figured that would bring out some talent," Sheriff Manson said. "You still have your outfit intact?"

"One of my best men split off on his

own. He's working farther west. I'm down to five men and me now. Go after a whole gang one man can't do the job right."

"Reasonable. You think this gang is in Dodge?"

"Possible. I saw the same Wanted couple of weeks ago, so I sent a letter to that sheriff down in Texas with him to send a return letter here at Dodge. Got back a good description of each of the jail breakers. All six of them. The one called the Professor should be the easiest to spot. Tall, well dressed, even went to college. Smooth talker. He's the one I'm looking for. Find him, find the rest."

"Seems reasonable. These guys wanted dead or alive?"

"The way I remember it."

The sheriff dropped into his chair. "You think they might be around here?"

"Bank got robbed down south along the trail from here to New Mexico. Had all the signs of being a job done by this Professor. He's smooth, slick, no gunplay, gets away before anyone knows the bank got busted open."

"So they might have come on up the trail to Dodge," the sheriff said.

"If the boot fits, Sheriff. . . ."

That noon Handshoe and his five men

covered every eating place in Dodge. Nowhere did they find a man who answered the description of the Professor. Twice the bounty hunters checked the hotel dining room while Willy Boy and Johnny Joe were having their midday dinner, but the hunters did not recognize them.

Handshoe called all of his men back to his hotel room in the afternoon and they went over the letter from Sheriff Jim Dunwoody of Oak Park, Texas. They memorized the descriptions of the other members of the Willy Boy Gang and by supper time they were out again checking the eating establishments.

Handshoe took the four hotels, starting at five in the evening, and coming to each of the four and spending fifteen minutes at each. He figured that should let him get back to the first one 45 minutes after he left it for a second look.

In the first hotel he spotted a man who dressed well, had a well tended beard and was eating at a table alone. He was devouring the most expensive meal on the menu. Handshoe gave the waitress a dollar bill and asked her who the man was.

She was young and giggled and said he was the most handsome man she'd ever seen.

"His name, does he have a name?" Handshoe asked.

She promised to find out and five minutes later came back.

"The desk clerk says he's J. Ambrose Collier. He's here buying horses to sell to the army. Isn't he handsome?"

Handshoe shooed her away and moved to the next hotel. He figured the white Indian would be easy to spot. Long hair, maybe a braid, dark features, wary? But no such person showed up in any of the four hotel dining rooms. Nor did the Mexican. There were some small cafes where both those men would be more likely to eat.

When Handshoe checked the first hotel again just before six, he grinned. The young man sitting at the second table was 17 or 18. The man who sat across from him was older and much larger. Could be Willy Boy and the big man in the group, what was his name . . . Gunner Johnson.

When they stood to leave, Handshoe caught his breath. The small young man was no more than five-feet five, maybe five-six. His companion was at least six-feet two-inches and solid, maybe 240 pounds.

Handshoe felt his hands tremble. There was $4,000 on the hoof! He should take them right then and get the other four as he could find them. But he waited. He wanted all six of them together!

He left the dining room before they did and waited in the lobby. They went up the stairs and he followed far enough behind not to be noticed. He saw the small man go into a room on the second floor, room 22. Gunner went up to the third floor and Handshoe lost him.

Handshoe went at once to the front desk and talked to the clerk. He took a room on the second floor and checked to see if he could open his door a crack and see room 22. He couldn't, so he went downstairs with the numbers of four rooms that would serve his purpose. One of them was vacant, so he rented it for two nights and went up there and began his watch.

There would be somebody watching that room now 24-hours a day just as soon as he could contact his men. Right then he couldn't leave because he might miss something. Willy Boy wouldn't wiggle without Handshoe knowing about it. He grinned. He could almost feel all those green dollar bills in his hands. $12,000! He'd take them all dead if he could. Then all he would have to do was ride back to Texas and pick up the money in trade for the death certificates.

Willy Boy left his room about an hour later and went to a saloon where he bought two bottles of cold beer and got into a game of three card monte. A short time later a man came in and joined him. The man was a Mexican. He spoke with Willy Boy and slipped out.

Handshoe followed him. This would be Juan Romero. Yes, he would take out Romero now and stash him in the jail. Then get the rest of them as they contacted Willy Boy tonight. Obviously they weren't going to hold a meeting so he could get them all at once.

He hurried to catch up with Romero and in a dark spot between splashes of light from saloons, he pushed his revolver into Romero's side.

"Don't make a move or say a word, Romero, or you're a dead man looking for a graveyard." Handshoe felt the Mexican tighten up, then relax.

"Who are you?"

"No matter, you're one of the Willy Boy Gang, and I'm here to collect the $2,000 on you dead or alive. Make it easy for me, try to get away."

He felt the Mexican sag then, give up completely. He'd seen it happen before.

There were a lot of good ways to take the fight out of a man.

"Just walk easy right down to the jail house. We'll stash you in there all peaceful like and you live another month or so before you hang. Might even see your wife and kids. You must have about six or eight."

Handshoe walked beside Romero, his left hand holding the Mexican's right arm above the elbow, his right hand jamming the big .45 into his ribs.

"Nice and easy like and we won't wake up the natives." Handshoe felt Romero's arm tighten and he jammed the gun harder into his side.

"No tricks, greaser, or I'll blow you in half! Once Michael Handshoe and his team of bounty hunters gets a man, he never gets away. Remember that, Romero."

Romero looked at him then and nodded but at the same time his balled fist slammed into Handshoe's crotch, then upward at the deadly .45 in his own ribs.

Handshoe felt the blow crush his testicles and the pain daggered through him before he could pull the trigger. Romero's lightning like upward thrust of his arm swept the muzzle of the weapon up and away from his side.

When the impulses got through from Handshoe's pain fogged brain to his finger to pull the trigger, the weapon went off pointing almost straight up. The scream of pain tore into the night air from Handshoe's mouth. Romero grabbed the cylinder so it couldn't turn, which meant it couldn't fire again. He bent the weapon backwards until he heard a finger bone snap and another braying scream of pain from Handshoe.

He let go of the weapon and Juan Romero stood there as Handshoe fell to the ground holding his genitals, pulling his knees up to relive some of the torturous pain.

Then Romero ran. He figured some of the men would be in their hotel rooms. He pounded on Willy Boy's door first and told him what happened. They rushed to the other rooms. Gunner and Johnny Joe and Eagle were in their rooms. Only the Professor was not there.

They all packed at once. Willy Boy kicked open the Professor's locked door and packed his gear and they sauntered downstairs and out the back door.

They had left their horses at the livery and now three of them filtered that way to saddle all six horses. Juan, Willy Boy and

Gunner began to work the saloons to find the one that held the Professor.

After ten minutes they found him in a saloon sweet talking a dance hall girl into flipping on her back for him for free.

A whispered word to the Professor from Willy Boy and the bank robber patted the whore's little bottom and slipped out of the saloon.

The Willy Boy Gang hit leather and galloped out of town to the northeast along a good wagon road.

"Tell me again what he said," Willy Boy shouted at Juan. The Mexican rode up beside him and went over what happened and what the man had said.

"Bounty hunter? Michael Handshoe? I've never heard of anyone by that name." He turned to the rest and shouted. "Any of you heard of a bounty hunter named Handshoe?"

"Oh, shit!" the Professor roared. "*Michael* Handshoe?" He rode in closer.

"That's what he called himself," Romero said.

"Double shit! Handshoe is the best bounty hunter in the plains states. He never goes after anybody until they are worth at least $1,000. The worst part is he has from six to ten men who ride with him. He's got

134

his own gang and he uses them to ride down lone men with paper out on them."

"Must have come to Dodge looking for us," Willy Boy said. "That damn poster is going to cause us trouble after all."

"How could he spot us from the poster?" Johnny Joe asked. "Weren't no descriptions of us on it."

"Guy like Handshoe probably wrote to Dunwoody and asked for descriptions," the Professor said. "Dunwoody would answer the same day and we aren't that far from Oak Park."

"So, he'll trail us," Willy Boy said.

"Damn right," the Professor agreed. "He's said to have the best tracker in the West who works for him. The tracker gets two shares of the reward. He's good."

"Eagle!" Willy Boy called. "Get your redskin ass up here. How do we mess up our trail to confuse Handshoe and his tracker?"

Eagle grinned in the soft moonlight. "Follow me." He turned his mount around and rode back along the same trail they had ridden out. After half a mile he stopped.

"Now we split up in six directions. See the north star? We all ride east and west in a big arc and we always swing a little

135

north. When we hit the first creek, you on the left ride downstream. Those on the right, ride upstream until we meet. When Handshoe's trackers follow us in the morning, they'll fan out following our trails. Make it three or five miles of an arc on each side and one man goes straight north.

"We'll be waiting for the Handshoe rider who tracks straight north. He'll get there two hours before the others. We pick him off, and then the next man who arrives alone. We pick them off one at a time until none are left."

Willy Boy grinned. "Anyone have any suggestions?"

Professor nodded. "Yeah. First stream is the Buckner about 20 miles north of here. I've been in this area before. Let's not get lost. First man riding north gets there in about five hours. The rest of us won't find that man for eight or nine hours."

Willy looked at his crew. "Johnny Joe, you go straight north and take it easy. Eagle, you take the widest circle to the left. I'll take the widest one to the right, the rest of you space in between. Remember, we all meet at the stream and work down and upstream until we find Johnny Joe. Then we figure out our ambush."

He looked at Eagle. "Will it work?"

"Damn right! I seen a cavalry troop cut to pieces that way a squad at a time. I couldn't believe they didn't catch on to the trick."

Again they rode.

They had left Dodge about eight o'clock, Willy Boy estimated. By the time they split up it must have been nearly nine. As Willy Boy looked up at the north star and the big dipper in its nightly circle around it, he decided it was about ten o'clock. He'd been riding an hour. He had a long night's ride ahead of him.

As he rode he couldn't help thinking about bounty hunters. How could they do that? How could they go out and hunt down other men and bring them back dead or alive for a reward? If they were lawmen that was different. Such work was a lawman's job, his duty, but for a civilian to do it — it just wasn't right.

The whole hour of thinking about bounty hunters reinforced Willy Boy's hatred of the breed, and made him more determined than ever to find the one named Deeds Conover.

# Chapter Eleven

It *was* nearly four in the A.M. before Willy Boy rode down the creek and found where the other men had gathered. He was the last one in. Everyone else but Eagle had rolled out blankets and gone to sleep.

Eagle showed him where they had hidden the horses in heavy brush so they couldn't be seen from the south. They went back to the south side of the brush and stared in the direction of Dodge.

"Only one way I see that it won't work," Willy Boy said. "That's if this Handshoe has seen the trick before, or if he figures even with the spread out trails, everyone is going to come together somewhere in the north so he puts all of his men on the true north trail."

"Won't happen," Eagle said. "His tracker will talk him out of that. He'll point out that we may have scattered for good, and be out on our own. By following just one trail, he'd lose all except one man."

"Keep hoping," Willy Boy said and spread his blanket. "If you can't sleep,

138

Eagle, stay up until dawn and then wake me. Should be a couple of hours. Then we'll figure out our ambush and we'll put Johnny Joe on guard."

By seven o'clock the next morning they had cooked their breakfast and settled on the ambush positions. The smoke from the fire would be well dissipated in the four or five hours it would take anyone from the Handshoe bounty group to find them.

They spread the ambush out with all six of them on a line in the heavier brush. Each man had cut a firing zone in front of him, but it was decided that they would take the man without firing a shot, if possible.

That would allow no sound of shots to warn the others. Eagle went up a heavily leafed tree directly over the track that Johnny Joe used to come into the brush. If the tracker came that way, and wasn't frightened by the brush line, there was a chance. Eagle would go up the tree at the first sight of a single rider coming toward them.

After that, everyone dozed off except Johnny Joe who kept watch. Before he slept, Willy Boy plotted it out. If Handshoe and his men had left at daylight, it might have taken them an hour to find their tracks. Then by seven they could be on the way.

He figured the first man could come up Johnny Joe's tracks no sooner than eleven to eleven-thirty. He had instructed Johnny Joe to wake up everyone at eleven.

"We have a visitor," Johnny Joe said when he shook Willy Boy awake at eleven o'clock. Willy Boy stood in the brush and spotted a lonesome rider coming toward them, head lowered, watching the trail Johnny Joe had made the night before.

Eagle stepped up and grinned. "Old Indian trick work pretty good on white eyes," he said.

"Get up your tree, redskin," Willy Boy said. "Use that skinning knife you keep so sharp. I don't want to hear this bastard even give a death rattle."

They waited. It was nearly a half hour after they saw the rider that he came near the brush. He looked around in all directions, then shrugged and walked his mount forward. He came straight down Johnny Joe's trail, then saw an open area 50 yards downstream and angled that way.

"Damn," Willy Boy whispered. He could see Eagle in the tree. He motioned for him to come down and to get downstream and get the man. Eagle crawled down the tree without a sound and faded into the brush and trees working his way down the creek.

For five minutes they heard nothing, then a strangled scream began and stopped quickly.

Two minutes later and Eagle stepped out from behind a large cottonwood and grinned.

"Don't worry, white eyes, your faithful Indian friend has saved the day again for you. Subtract one bounty hunter."

"You took care of his horse and the body?" Willy Boy asked him.

"Yes. I'm going up the tree. I can see out farther from up there."

Ten minutes later Eagle called softly. "We've got a pair coming in from the right. Looks like they're riding together. Might never have split up."

"We'll take out these two any way we can. Pistols if they get close enough, or rifles while they're not up to the brush. Let's use the rifles. Make sure they get to within a hundred yards, then use those Henrys. I'll give the word to fire."

The bounty hunters came closer as they tracked the other horses now. There should be showing two or three sets of prints. They did not seem afraid of the brushline.

Eagle kept watching to the left. So far nothing showed.

The two riders came closer, stared for a moment at the brush and trees they were following, then rode on. A dozen strides later they were at the hundred yard mark that Willy Boy had set up by eye.

He sighted in on the rider closest to the trees. "Now!" he said firmly. He refined his sight and squeezed the trigger. The second his shot sounded three more rounds went off and both men on the horses were blown out of their saddles. One tried to crawl to the brush but Willy Boy yelled at him to stop or he'd be killed.

Willy Boy ran up to the downed man, kicked away his gun and scowled at the bounty hunter who bled from a chest wound.

"How many men does Handshoe have with him?" Willy Boy demanded.

The man shrugged. "Don't matter to me none. Started with five and Handshoe. How many you killed?"

"Three, including you. You after the reward?"

"Yeah, just the reward. Only my second try."

"Well, better luck in hell," Willy Boy said and watched as the man gasped for breath, gushed up a mouthful of blood and his face fell forward directly into the red life fluid as it soaked into the ground. He shuddered once, then his right hand lifted and dropped as a death rattle whispered out of his lungs.

"Leave them where they lay and picket their horses here," Willy Boy ordered.

He wrote a note message on a small notebook he carried and folded the paper, then put it in the hand of the man who had just died. He changed his mind, unfolded the paper so it couldn't be missed.

The note read: "Give it up, Handshoe, unless you want to join these three men of yours in hell." He signed it Willy Boy and they pushed across the creek and rode.

"Think he'll still come after us?" Gunner asked.

"Hell, yes," Willy Boy said. "We hurt him, but we hurt his pride more. He might slow down and hire some more men, but he'll try for us again, you can bet on it."

Willy Boy scowled. "Bounty hunters are the scum of the earth, the dregs of a sewer. They're the worst human beings on the face of the earth!"

It was only four o'clock when Willy Boy called a halt along a little stream and he talked to Juan. "Cook us up a good supper,

Juan, what do you have?"

"Not much, we left town too fast to buy any trail supplies."

Eagle watched them. "Plan on a rabbit stew," he said, and took his Henry rifle and walked into the prairie.

Juan dug a hole and fixed a pot of beans to cook the way Eagle had done before, but it wouldn't be ready until the next morning. Gunner came back from where he had been standing guard.

"Don't see anybody coming either way. We must not be on the main trail."

"Fact is, we aren't," Willy Boy said. "We probably should turn off to the east and work toward one of the towns."

"Towns mean trouble for us," Johnny Joe said. "Give me another few days and I'll be able to do my part."

"Everybody is doing fine," Willy Boy said quickly. "Damn, we're still free of that jail. Nobody's got hung. Only one of us got shot up. We're doing great. Juan, I know you want to get down to Mexico. One of these days we'll turn that direction. 'Course, then we'll probably lose you to your wife and kids."

They heard a shot and everyone hunkered down. "Eagle," Willy Boy said. "He just shot our supper."

Eagle came back a few minutes later with an eight pound jack rabbit over his shoulder. He skinned out the rabbit, then cleaned it and cut it up in one of Romero's cooking pots. From a pocket he pulled out eight wild onions about the size of an egg. From the other pocket he brought a dozen small apples.

"Wild onions and crab apples. Boil the apples for about twenty minutes and they'll taste like honey. The onions can go in the pot with the rabbit stew and the potatoes. Next time we'll raid some farmer's garden and do better."

Eagle hovered over where Willy Boy sat cleaning his Henry rifle.

"Willy Boy, you went to see the army folks at Fort Dodge. What did they say about the Fourteenth?"

"You sure I went? We didn't have much time there."

"You went, I followed you part way. Where is the Fourteenth stationed?"

"I really didn't want to tell you, Eagle," Willy Boy said. "I was afraid you might take off for the place and get yourself shot full of holes."

"So you found out?"

"Yes. The Lieutenant back at the fort said that the Fourteenth Cavalry Regiment

145

was assigned to Fort Boise, way up in Idaho."

"How far is that?"

"How far? Halfway across the continent from here. It's at least 1,200 miles. At 40 miles a day, it would take you 30 days just to ride that far, provided you didn't get lost."

"Let's go out there," Eagle said. "I want to pay them back, but I like to have a bunch of men working with me. Let's go."

"Hey, hey, easy. This is my bunch. I still give the orders. Right now we're looking for Deeds Conover, the bastard who killed my Pa. After we get him we'll go after the bastards who murdered your family. Fair enough?"

Eagle scowled for a moment. He walked around the cooking fire and added some sticks to it. When he came back he nodded.

"Fair is fair. I'll wait for you."

"Good, when is that rabbit stew going to be done?" Willy Boy asked.

About an hour later as they ate the rabbit stew, chewing the cooked meat off the bones, Willy Boy asked Gunner how he came to be in jail.

Gunner shook his head. "No, I don't tell nobody."

Willy Boy handed him more of the stew and the big man thanked Willy Boy who had stood up for him twice in the jail at Oak Park. He couldn't deny Willy Boy what he wanted.

"Well, I worked in a livery stable in Suttler Town. I did good on the horses. They seem to like me. I was working and the boss wasn't around when somebody came in to rent a horse.

"He was a big man and mean and he kept yelling at me to rush, to hurry up . . . I was doing it as fast as I could and I told him and he took a punch at me and knocked me down and everybody laughed at me.

"I got a good memory. Two nights later I was in the saloon watching the girls and having a beer and the same big guy came in and started drinking.

"I got madder and madder at him. I never did drink much and I bought some whiskey and next thing I knew I ran at this guy and knocked him down and kicked him. When he got up I knocked him down again, then I grabbed his neck and squeezed it and I guess I nearly killed him.

"Somebody hit me on the head with a bottle and I passed out. I woke up in jail and then they had a trial that lasted about ten minutes, and then I met you guys."

The Professor growled. "They had you pegged as a hardened, vicious criminal. They sentenced you to ten years for that?"

"No, fifteen years, with good behavior," Gunner said. "I . . . I never really meant to hurt the man. But that's why I don't drink at all now. No more."

"Nobody is going to put you in jail again, Gunner," Eagle said. "All five of us will see to that."

"So we'll find a town over east aways, and get back to hunting Deeds Conover," Willy Boy said. "He's got to be around here somewhere."

"What if we don't find him?" Johnny Joe asked. "We can't just go wandering around here forever."

"Two weeks," Willy Boy said. "Two more weeks we look for him, then we decide about Idaho or Mexico or whatever somebody else got to do. Agreed?"

They all nodded.

"Agreed. Now, best we get some sleep if'n we gonna do some hard riding tomorrow. We need to find that town to buy some trail food. Besides, I got to send a letter to Frank Galloway back in Oak Park, Texas. I owe that man five dollars."

# Chapter Twelve

*Michael Handshoe* looked down at the two men near the brush lined stream. He swung off his horse to make sure both were dead. The piece of paper in the one's hand caught his attention. He squatted and pulled the paper from dead fingers.

Handshoe read it, crumpled it and started to throw it away, then he smoothed it out and put it in his pocket. He needed more troops now, that was obvious. His last two men came riding toward him. They were a quarter of a mile off.

Damnit! He had been right. He had wanted to charge up the due north trail, but his tracker had talked him out of it. It had been a sucker play and he fell for it. Somebody in the Willy Boy bunch was damn smart, and Handshoe didn't think it was the leader. Eagle, the Comanche Indian. He would be the designer of this trap.

The men rode up to him, eyes wide, looking at the bodies.

"Take a look around," he told them after

they had looked their fill at the two bodies. "Bastards tricked us. See if you can find Lars. He came up the short route, should have been here first."

"Damn, here first and dead first, I'll wager," one of the newer men said. He angled downstream and began searching through the brush. The other man went upstream.

Handshoe hunkered down and drew lines in the dirt with a stick. He had been out-thought, out-maneuvered and out-gunned. Damn!

"Found him!" the downstream men bellowed. "Dead."

"Bring him back up here with his horse if it's there."

Handshoe made the decision quickly. He had to take these men back to town and bury them, write letters to next of kin, hire six or eight new men and get back on the bastards' trail. In ten years he'd never come up against a gang this tough or this vicious. But he'd take them.

It took him two days to get his business done and back on the trail. He hired seven new men, made them prove they could hit what they shot at with pistol and rifle. Then he bought them all identical low crowned white hats and they headed out.

They joked about being Handshoe's army, but in fact that's what they were. An army of ten men who did what he told them to, and fought for money.

They came to the site of the ambush and his new tracker picked up the gang's trail quickly.

"All six of them moving steady to the east," the tracker said. His name was Harry but everyone called him Loco. "There's a town or two over that way. From what you said, they left Dodge sudden without supplies."

They rode hard and three hours later could see two small towns ahead, one north and the other south. Handshoe sent three men to the one farthest away. They were to talk first to the storeman and see if six men bought trail supplies. If they didn't find them there they should check the hotel and the saloons. If they found no trace, they were to high tail it back to the second town.

Handshoe took the rest of his men into the closer town. When they rode in he saw it was about 200 people strong, had five or six stores, no railroad or main trail. The general store owner said he'd sold a lot of trail supplies to two men who came in. He described them. One was a Mexican who spoke good English and the other one was a big guy, over six feet and sturdy who seemed quiet, maybe a little slow witted.

"When did you sell the goods?" Handshoe asked impatiently.

The store owner took off a scuffy bill cap and scratched his head through thinning hair. "Reckon it was three days ago. Same day the Younger boy broke his leg. Yep, three days ago."

"You see which direction they rode out?"

"Nope. Had lots of business that day, and a supply wagon brought in my order from Chicago."

Handshoe thanked him and they rode down the street. The hotel wouldn't be any help. The town whores might if the Willy Boy bunch talked as they pleasured. Long chance there. Handshoe unfolded a map of that section of Kansas he had bought at Dodge and looked for the main trails and the next town.

What was this bunch after? What was motivating them? He knew they all broke out of jail together. Why hadn't this bunch split up and vanished into the West? They all could fade into the wilderness and never be heard of again. Staying together they made themselves a bigger target. One that he would track down. For a $12,000 payoff he could do the job right.

Right now he decided they thought staying together would help them stave off any posse that came after them. It had worked twice so far, and had whipped him in the first meeting. But it wouldn't be the last. They had trail supplies, what would they do now?

Handshoe tried to put himself in their shoes. The kid could still be looking for Deeds Conover. Conover was a real bastard, a shoot first type who caused the profession trouble, gave all bounty hunters a bad name.

How do you hunt for a bounty hunter? Easy, you check with every lawman you can find and ask if the man has been around. Makes it harder when you're also on a wanted poster yourself. They would send in the man who would be suspected least. Maybe Willy Boy himself looking for his daddy, maybe. He'd say his daddy just happened to be Deeds Conover.

Towns, he'd work every town he came to. There were three of them within the next ten miles as they came into a slightly more settled section of the Kansas plains.

He took the most likely town and sent three men to each of the other two. They would meet in the center spot later in the day to report.

He got the men moving and set a fast pace.

"We're on their trail again, but three days behind them. So we have to make that up. We'll be riding until midnight every day. Checking all of these towns will take more time, but we have no choice. I want to get that little bastard!"

When the three teams met late that day, two reported that there had been a person inquiring about Deeds Conover. One of the men was small and young asking for his father. In the other town the man had been tall, well dressed, well spoken and pleasant. They pegged him as the Professor. The lawmen hadn't heard of Conover.

The next town ahead was no problem. It was over 20 miles along the main trail toward Hutchinson.

"We'll be riding a long time tonight, so we better get a meal while we're in town," Handshoe told his men. They all had big steak dinners and two pieces of pie. Then they got back on the trail.

True to his word, Handshoe pushed them until almost midnight before they bedded down. The next town was only a few miles away. They didn't even know its name. One of these little Kansas towns was starting to look like the rest of them.

Handshoe thought through the odds of making any money on this challenge. The $12,000 potential was still there. He could afford to give it a month's try. If it didn't work, he'd have to work on some cases that would bring in some money.

Willy Boy and his men had been to six different towns. None of the lawmen that Willy Boy and the Professor talked to had heard anything of Deeds Conover for a year or more.

The leader of the gang was getting discouraged. He wanted results and he wanted them now. Patience had never been one of his major character traits.

They rode into Grand Prairie at dusk, rented rooms at the small hotel by twos the way they always did, and then Willy Boy checked with the town marshall.

Willy Boy walked into the lawman's office with a touch of uneasiness as he usually tried to do. He held his black hat in his hand and combed at his wild hair with his fingers.

A man behind a counter looked up.

"Yeah, kid?"

"Looking for my Pa. He been around here?"

The lawman laughed. "Help a bit if I knew the man's name."

"Oh, yeah. He's Deeds Conover. He been here lately?"

"Conover, the bounty hunter?"

"I guess that's what he does. He travels a lot."

"Figures. Yeah, he was through here yesterday, matter of fact. On the trail of a guy called Yellow Charlie, whoever the hell he is. Guy by that moniker been living out of town a mile or two. Never did find out what the hell happened when the bounty hunter went out there."

"Gosh, that's great. Where can I find this Yellow Charlie's place?"

The lawman looked at him a minute, then shrugged. "Might not be too healthy out there for a while. I hear this Conover gent is kind of rough on guys wanted by the law."

"He's my Pa. I want to find him."

"All right. Yellow Charlie lives about eight miles out of town on a little creek called West River. Kind of a horse ranch, last I knew. Some corrals and a small house. Go out the north road to the third mile marker, then east for three more and you should be almost there."

Willy nodded. "Thank you kindly, sir. I

appreciate this." He turned and hurried out of the office.

Back at the hotel he called the five men around him and told them what he'd learned. It was dark by then.

"We going out now?" Gunner asked.

"Right now," Willy Boy said. "Bring your rifles and six-guns and plenty of ammo and all your gear. We might not be back this way. But remember, when we capture the bastard, I'm the one who gets to finish him. Anybody kills him first and I'll be damn mad."

It was an easy place to find. Kansas had been marked off in mile square sections. Not all the roads were in yet, but the markers were up in this county every mile. When they came to the end of the three miles east they could see the start of some breaks and a small hill. They rode toward it and came on the small ranch a mile farther on.

At first glance it seemed to be unoccupied. But then they saw the faint glow of what must be a candle through the one small window. The house was old, poorly made. It looked like it might have been a soddy at one time that was fixed up and given wooden walls and wood roof instead of good Kansas sod.

They watched but could see no movement. Willy Boy had stopped the horses well back and they had walked up to where they could see better. Now he took Eagle and they slipped toward the cabin without a sound.

Willy Boy edged up to the high window and looked inside through the spots and sheen of dirt. It was a candle burning on a wooden chair. On another chair, facing the window, a man had been tied. It was a journeyman job for any sailor, knots tight, only a little rope used, no slack. No way to escape.

Nowhere else in the room that he could see, was there another person or any sign of another. There had to be someone else there to tie up the man.

Eagle took a look and then they edged back where they could whisper.

"Got to be another man in there," Eagle said. "We can't see in. Should we jump inside with shotguns ready?"

"Damn, I don't know. If that man is Yellow Charlie, then Deeds Conover could be in there sleeping. He might be outside taking a piss, or he could be riding back to town for some supplies before he brings in this wanted man."

"I know there's another man in there," Eagle said.

"Let's go back and talk it over. We've got nothing to lose. We can take him anytime."

The Professor listened to what they had seen and what they figured might be the situation.

"What if the man tied in the chair is Deeds Conover?" the Professor asked. "Maybe Yellow Charlie captured Conover."

"Guy tied up didn't remind me of Conover," Willy Boy said.

"It's been over three years since you saw him. Did the man in the chair have yellow hair?"

"No," Eagle said.

"Damn! I didn't notice that," Willy Boy said. "So what the hell should we do now?"

Juan spoke up. "Scare whoever is in there. Put six rifle slugs through the window. Then when the noise dies down, tell the men inside to come out with their hands on top of their heads."

Willy Boy grinned. "Yeah, I like that. Safe, strong, should work." He positioned the men to surround the cabin, then kept Eagle with him and they both pumped three slugs through the window as quickly as they could lever fresh .52 caliber rounds into the Henrys.

The silence following the shots sounded louder than the firing.

"Come out of there with your hands up," Willy Boy bellowed in his toughest voice. "We've got ten men around this cabin. You can't get away. Come out now or we'll burn the place down."

There was no reaction from anyone in the cabin for a moment, then the cabin door opened and a barking dog jolted through and into the darkness. A pistol cracked and the dog stopped barking and slinked away in the night.

"You've got fifteen seconds, then we burn you out!" Willy Boy shouted.

The door swung open again and a small man shuffled out into the pale moonlight. His hands were over his head. He wasn't more than five feet tall. He stood there squinting into the darkness.

"Who the hell are you?" Willy Boy brayed.

"Who the hell's asking?" the old cracking voice shot back.

Willy Boy laughed. "I'm Willy Boy and I'm hunting one Deeds Conover. That him you have tied up inside?"

"Not even by a hard lick. That young coot is my nephew and I'm trying to show him how to tie up a man so he can't noway get free. Want to take a look?"

"Already looked through the window," Willy Boy said. "You can put your hands down now. You know a bounty man name of Deeds Conover is on your trail?"

"Hell yes, think I'm blind? He drew down on me yesterday and shot close to my foot and I gived up."

"So why didn't he take you in for the bounty?"

The old man laughed. "Hail, son, I'm only a two-fifty paper. Got a paper myself to prove it, and it's from almost nine years ago. Doubt if it's any good now. Told this jasper that and offered him $20 to move on."

"What'd he do?" Eagle asked.

"Do, he took my twenty, stole another twenty I had in a tabakky can, and rode off after I fed him supper last night. Any more fool questions?"

"Guess not, old man."

"Good, I got one. You owe me fifty cents to put a new pane of glass in that little winder. When you gonna pay me for it? You're about the third varmint who has shot it out on me."

Willy Boy chuckled. "Guess you're right. I had no call to destroy your property that way." He stood. "Don't shoot, I'm walking up to give you a dollar. I don't got nothing smaller right now."

"Dollar's fine," the old man said. "Lonnie, don't shoot this gent. He's paying for the winder."

The young man who had been tied up stepped into the door frame with his uncle, a long gun in his hand.

The old man turned. "How'n hell you get loose?"

A half hour later, the Willy Boy Gang camped down on the little creek. They had found no sign of the bounty hunter's camp.

"Come morning we try to pick up his tracks. Should be one horse moving fast. He's working this area. Chances are he'll hit the next town east and look over the Wanteds. We'll try to meet up with him. Goddamn, but we're getting close, Professor. Getting damn close to that bastard Conover!"

# Chapter Thirteen

It *was* three days and seven small towns later that they had another report of Deeds Conover. The sheriff at Burnt Oak said he had been through there the day before, sniffed through the Wanteds and then asked about a local who used to be a bounty man.

"Do you remember who the local man was, Sheriff?" Willy Boy asked.

"Sure, Josh Lenton. He's a boot and shoe man now. Makes some of the best boots I've ever worn. Got a little shop down the street about six doors."

Willy Boy talked to Josh.

"Yep, Deeds was here. I never was a friend of that man, but I knew him. Even worked with him on one case and we split the reward, but never again. I told him so. He's mostly just roaming around, trying to find something to work on. Used to be we'd go to a judge or sheriff and get a Wanted and go out after that man. Deeds isn't working that way now."

"Any idea where he went?"

"Said he was going to the hotel. Reckon

he's still there. I know he ordered three girls from the Lucky Lady Saloon for the night. He might be up by now since it's almost noon."

"Thanks, Josh. When I need some new boots, I'll come back and get them from you."

Willy Boy walked out of the store and directly to the hotel.

"Checked out?" the room clerk said with surprise. "Oh, no, not Mr. Conover. He said he'd probably be here for a week. He's up in room 301. That's in the corner on the third floor."

Willy Boy thanked him and went up the stairs quietly. There was no one in the hall on the third floor and Willy Boy put his ear to room 301 and listened. All he heard were giggles and a man growling some words he couldn't understand.

Willy Boy wished he had one of the sawed off shotguns. All he had was his .45 with five shots. That would have to do. He stepped back from the door against the far hall wall, drew the .45, took two steps and jumped at the door with all his 130 pounds of weight behind his boot.

It landed on the door right beside the door handle and popped open the lock, smashing the door inward until it slammed against the wall. Willy Boy nearly fell but kept his feet. He jumped inside the room and saw naked bodies entangled on the big bed.

A man's face lifted from the tangle and stared at him.

"What the hell are you doing?" the man roared.

There was no mistake, it was Deeds Conover, the same man who had shot-gunned his father.

"Deeds Conover?" Willy Boy demanded, the .45 leveled at the man's head from six feet away.

"Maybe, maybe not, so what?"

Willy Boy stared at the crooked face, with one eye slightly lower than the other, the jaw that sagged a little to the same side as if someone had mashed in half of his face a little. Dangerous dark eyes stared out at him. The man had black hair and a heavy beard showing stubble.

"You're Deeds Conover all right. I saw you shotgun my Pa over in Missouri three years ago, and right now I'm gonna kill you."

He fired just as Conover dove back into the mass of naked arms, legs, torsos, and three women's frightened faces.

"Get out of here, ladies, or you're dead!"

Willy Boy shouted.

One squirmed off the bed on one side and a second one on the other side, but the man held fast to the third one covering most of his naked body.

"You wouldn't shoot an innocent woman!" the man shouted.

"Damn right I will, gladly!" Willy Boy screamed at him. He fired again, grazing the man's shoulder over the bare shoulder of the woman.

The woman screamed. The two girls who had jumped off the bed grabbed clothes and rushed out of the room into the hall.

"Now, calm down, whoever you are," the man said. "You've made a mistake. I'm not that man you're looking for."

Willy Boy found a hairy leg unprotected and he fired again, the slug boring through the man's calf and he bellowed in pain.

Then in a surprise move the man surged upward and threw the naked woman at Willy Boy. She hit him in the chest, knocking him backwards. He dropped his gun and the woman fell on top of him as the man jumped up, kicked Willy twice in the side, grabbed his pants and ran out of the room.

By the time Willy Boy got untangled

from the nude woman and found his gun, Deeds Conover was gone out of the hall. He tried doors along the way. Most were locked, two were empty. In another one a woman screamed at him. He ran down to the second floor and checked the empty rooms, but Deeds Conover didn't seem to be around.

He went back to the man's room. The last woman had dressed and hurried out. He found the man's gear. In one shirt pocket was a letter addressed to Deeds Conover, General Delivery, Dodge, Kansas. He had the right man.

But he let him get away. He went over every item that Conover owned in the room. He found only a .44 pistol, an 1868 Springfield rifle, and a purse with $20 in it. He took the weapons and the purse and sat in an empty room halfway down the hall with the door barely cracked open so he could watch the room Conover had used.

Conover would not leave his bag of clothes and weapons and head out of town. By midnight, Willy Boy considered that he may have misjudged Deeds Conover.

He checked at the livery stable and found that Mr. Conover had paid his bill and ridden out about three that afternoon. He headed east, but that was no real test of his continuing direction.

Willy Boy found his crew, roused them out of bed, got Johnny Joe from a poker game and the Professor from a brothel and they rode east. By sun up they had covered more than 20 miles. They had not seen a campfire, smelled an unhoused smoke, or seen a single traveler.

It had been a fool's ride, Willy Boy knew. But he had to do something. They found a brushy area near the main road and camped out of sight. One man stood guard watching for the sight of a lone man on a sorrel. The livery stable man had told him it was a sorrel and easy to spot.

"We must have come past him in the night," Willy Boy said.

Three lone riders came along the road, but none of them could be Conover. One was past 60, the other two were kids of 15.

By noon, Willy Boy decided they were still behind him. They rode hard for the next town, Wagon Bend. It was on a curve of a fair sized river.

The town marshall said he hadn't seen anyone asking about wanted posters for two months.

The next town was smaller but there a man had looked through the wanted posters. He gave his name as Harry

Charles, but he fit Conover's description.

"Yep, left here about two hours ago. I didn't exactly believe him as we talked. He headed out of town to the west. I was curious enough to walk down to the edge of the hardware store and I saw him make a circle around the town and get back on the road going east. Next town is eight miles away."

They rode again, rumbling along at six miles to the hour in a jolting lope that was good for the horses, but not the best for the men. If they rode four hours at six miles an hour they should catch him if he was two hours ahead riding at four miles an hour.

It should have worked out that way, but Deeds Conover stopped in the town of Moorville to buy some trail food and gear. He was in that town when Willy Boy left the previous one. Conover spent nearly an hour having dinner and buying food and pots to use on his travels.

With that element thrown in, Willy Boy and his gang caught up with Deeds Conover about three that afternoon. They saw him a quarter-of-a-mile ahead, the white mane and tail of his horse easy to spot against the reddish brown color of the sorrel. Willy Boy and Eagle took off at a gallop after him.

The other horses were not as fast and the two led them by 100 yards after a brief stint. Deeds must have been watching his back trail because he at once spurred his horse off the road into a field and near a small stream with lots of brush and trees along it. He vanished into the trees, and Willy Boy and Eagle thundered along to where he entered the woods and charged after him.

Eagle held up his hand and they both stopped. Ahead they could hear brush cracking and branches breaking.

"I'll go outside in the clear area and ride ahead of him and wait for him," Eagle shouted. Willy Boy nodded and rode forward, his sawed off shotgun up and ready, both barrels loaded.

He went slower than he wanted to, but caution held him back. He didn't want to ride into an ambush, but he had to keep pushing Conover forward.

The cat and mouse game lasted for half an hour before Willy Boy sighted the bounty hunter. It was one of those little bluffs that come out of nowhere, that rises up on the plains suddenly like a festering pimple on the thigh of a beautiful woman.

The soil must have been special because

every inch of that little hillock was swarmed over with trees and brush, with choke cherries and crab apples and wild berries.

Deeds Conover sat on his horse near the top of the 50 foot slope and fired a rifle. The slug sang through the air three feet from Willy Boy and he jolted the mount behind some cottonwoods and out of sight.

Willy Boy peered around the last tree and saw Conover working higher on the lump of land and behind the heavy cover. Willy Boy heard a sound behind him and whirled around scratching for his revolver, but it was Eagle on foot.

"I saw him. He's good. You ride like hell around to the far side of the hill. Must be some kind of a trail over there. I'm going up on foot. He's waiting for one of us to come up on horseback. I can slip through the low brush and he'll never see me. I'll drive him down into your gunsights."

Willy Boy watched Eagle. "Don't you dare kill the guy. Wound him if you want to, but he's my meat!"

"I got the message a long time ago, white eyes. Now move. I'll need your distraction to help me get across that skimpy cover out there."

Willy Boy rode hard then, charging from

cover to cover. Once he heard a rifle shot but it was far in back of him. He found the curve of the hill less than 50 yards down and a small tributary creek angled that way so he could stay in adequate cover. Soon he was almost directly behind where he had first seen the bounty hunter.

There had been no more shots. Willy Boy checked the chamber of his Henry, filled up the magazine and then sat on his horse near a good sized oak tree and waited.

Eagle took his time getting across the sparse cover area, but once into the heavier growth, he hurried, then stopped and listened. Twice he heard a horse snorting. He was being asked to do something he didn't want to do, like climb a steep bank.

Eagle jogged up the slope, not breaking a branch. He moved from cover to cover like a morning fog. When he was halfway up, he stopped and listened again. He could hear the horse blowing.

Close. He moved cautiously now, easing forward. Around the next small growth of hickory brush, he could see the horse, but not the man.

He moved again and the horse vanished. It had taken some steps down the hill. It didn't want to negotiate the steep downward climb. Eagle hurried then and got to the top where he saw the hoofprints in an open space. Then 30 yards below he saw the bounty hunter riding down the hill.

Eagle lifted the rifle. He should kill him. But to Willy Boy the man's death wasn't important, it was how he died that counted. Eagle shifted his sights to the man's right shoulder and squeezed off the round.

The crack of the Henry echoed through the hills and was followed with a scream of pain. Conover didn't slam off the saddle. Eagle gave him credit for that. The bounty hunter jolted forward, kept his seat and threw both arms around the frightened horse's neck and hung on as he slipped into heavy cover and out of sight.

"Damaged package coming down the hill," Eagle shouted into the clear afternoon air.

Eagle worked down the trail left by the horse. It had taken the path of gentle descent and here and there he cut across the switchbacks and came to the bottom but found no horse. He looked around, then ran into the brush until he came to the small creek.

The big horse Conover was riding went across the creek and on east. Where was Willy Boy?

There was no chance Eagle could catch the bounty hunter on foot. His own horse was a quarter of a mile away.

*Where was Willy Boy?*

"Willy Boy! Where are you? Willy Boy?"

Eagle felt a cold anger seeping into his brain. Something had happened to their leader. He ran down the creek to where it joined the other one and soon picked up a set of hoofprints heading toward him. Eagle turned around and began tracking the prints. They had to be Willy Boy's horse.

The prints bent around the edge of the little hill and followed the creek that branched off around the hill. It meandered a little and then entered some heavy brush. He saw the horse grazing 20 yards ahead. To the left, below a big oak with low hanging branches, he found Willy Boy. He was stretched out as if he were sleeping, his long gun on the ground six feet away.

Eagle ran and dropped to his knees beside the youth. He was breathing, he had a heartbeat. Eagle looked at him again. On the side of his head in the hairline was a knot the size of a chicken egg. Eagle grinned and went to the creek and wet his bandana and brought it back. He put it on

Willy Boy's forehead.

"What the hell?" he asked.

Willy Boy tried to sit up but fell back quickly. He blinked, then found Eagle and slowly his eyes focused.

"Eagle, what happened?"

"Don't know, small white eye. My guess is that you rode ahead when you were looking away and smacked into an oak limb. You hear me shoot the bounty hunter?"

"Yeah. And then you yelled something about a package. I saw Conover hugging his horse's neck and the horse charging down the hill. I needed a better firing spot."

"And clobbered yourself on that oak branch right back there. I put a rifle round into Conover's shoulder. He'll be hurting for a long time. But by now he's half a mile away and riding until he puts that horse down and dead."

"Let's go after him," Willy Boy said. "Got to get him before he slips away again."

"You want to go?" Eagle asked.

"Yes."

"Try to sit up."

Willy Boy pushed himself up, but his eyes went wide and he gasped and fell over to one side. He groaned and eased over on his back. "Damnit to hell, guess I ain't going anywhere for a while."

"Old Indian practice: never ride horse with big knot on your skull. Seeing it's almost dusk, we might as well camp right here."

# Chapter Fourteen

*Willy Boy* lay in thick leaf mulch which had cushioned his fall and looked up at Eagle. "Better get the rest of the men up here. Three pistol shots should do it."

Eagle shot in the air three times, and yelled a couple of times. He heard an answering shot, then ten minutes later the other four men rode into the small clearing around the big oak tree.

Eagle told them briefly what had happened.

"Wanna camp here?" Gunner asked.

Eagle watched Willy Boy. "Or do you want one of us to stay here with you and the rest chase down Conover and bring him back here. He's hurt, can't get far."

"No! No, I have to be in on the capture and the kill. No! We'll stay here and I'll be traveling by morning. Then we can still find the bastard and I'll enjoy myself for a couple of days remembering my Pa as I kill the son of a bitch."

They made camp and brought a cooking pot of water so Willy Boy could keep a cold, wet cloth on the bump on his head. It began going down an hour later and Willy Boy could sit up.

"I thought we had him," Willy Boy said. "It should have worked. If I hadn't been such a clumsy ox we would have captured him for sure. He was coming almost right at me. I'd have shot his horse and then run him down. He's not a man, he's a killing animal and I aim to put an end to his killing."

They didn't put out a guard that night. Willy Boy and Eagle figured they were far enough off the main trail that no one would find them. If they did, Eagle said he would hear them coming for a quarter-of-a-mile.

Morning broke bright and cloudless and they left with the dawn. Willy Boy still had a headache, but it seeped gradually away as Eagle tracked the horse Deeds Conover had been riding.

"Galloped for a quarter of a mile," Eagle reported a short time later. "Then he settled down to a steady walk and went back to the wagon road heading east. He could be 40 miles ahead of us by now. Once he hits a town and his tracks get messed up with lots of others, I won't be able to follow him."

"Damn him!" Willy Boy screamed. "Damn him to hell!" He rode up and down a short piece of road, jerking the mount around on the end of each dash. "What do I have to do to catch that bastard?"

He stopped near Eagle who shook his head. "Probably be lucky. The bad thing is we've used up some of our luck finding him these two times already."

They rode east. When they hit the first small town they spread out checking hotels, eateries, the livery and lawman in town. Nobody remembered seeing a man with a slightly lopsided face who was a bounty hunter.

At the far edge of town where they gathered, Willy Boy pointed on forward.

"He's got to work, got to get another man he thinks he can pull in. He likes this area. Maybe we can sniff out a trail on him again. We just have to be patient and hope that we can dig him out. At the next town we'll decide. Let's ride."

It was 12 miles to the next settlement. There were more struggling farms now and fewer cattle ranches. The towns showed stress and struggle as well. When they came into Larned on the Arkansas River they did a slow search, talking to store owners, the livery, the hotel people, and even the doctor and then the sheriff. Nobody had seen a sign of a man with a shot up shoulder who had a face slightly askew.

They took rooms at the hotel two by two, then ate, and Willy Boy said they could be on their own for the rest of the day and the night. He had some thinking to do. He was fully recovered from his conk on the head now and sat in the Quiet Tiger Saloon working on a pair of beers.

Gunner stayed close to Willy Boy, playing solitaire and sipping on a cold glass of water.

After more than an hour of contemplating his bad luck and the strangeness of the fates, Willy Boy hadn't come up with a single idea that he liked. He had half a dozen plans bouncing around in his head, everything from heading for Boise and the Fourteenth Cavalry Regiment to getting Juan Romero safely back to his people in Mexico.

He eyed his watch and decided on an early supper at the hotel dining room, which the room clerk said was the best eating in town. Tomorrow he would determine exactly what they would do. He hadn't ruled out the idea of taking out a couple more banks, then riding north to the Union Pacific railroad and taking the train out to Idaho, or as close as they could get. The idea interested him, but he wasn't sure yet.

Tomorrow, he'd talk with the men and decide. Yeah, he'd do it tomorrow.

Michael Handshoe had missed the detour Willy Boy and his men took out to the cabin where they shot out the window. But with his ten men spread across a 30 mile stretch of Kansas land, they swept in every other clue they could find about six men riding eastward.

Twice more they found inquiries about Deeds Conover with the local law. They pushed on. Seldom did they have any tracks to follow. Once they picked up what their half Indian scout said were six riders, but they wound up going into a small ranch where the men all worked as cowhands.

Handshoe kept on figuring that he was closing the gap, but he was still over two days behind. Willy Boy's Gang could go at any speed they wanted to, but Handshoe and his men had to move cautiously, not overlooking any chance that the gang had turned north or south, or perhaps even west. It was donkey work and he hated it, but that was how a real bounty hunter earned his pay.

They swept through central Kansas like a clean broom. Twice they found fresh scents. Once they found that not only had the Willy Boy Gang been in one town, but that Deeds Conover was there at the same time. Willy Boy was on a quest of his own. Good, Handshoe thought. They could slip up on him and shoot his bunch to pieces while Willy Boy was trying to get Conover. Perfect!

They were at a small town seven miles from Larned when they hit a hot scent. Willy Boy had checked for the bounty hunter with the sheriff, and they had also contacted the local doctor. They were looking for a man shot in the shoulder, a tall man with a lopsided face. Conover, that was him. Handshoe would never forget his face.

After talking to half the people in town, most agreed that the men who had asked about Conover had headed out of town toward Larned.

He sent riders to bring in the troops on the fringes of their search area. By ten o'clock that night he had his men gathered at the Kansan Hotel, seven miles from Larned. He briefed them completely.

They had been over it time and time again, but now he got down to specifics, giving them descriptions of each man and making them repeat it until each one could identify all of the men and call them by name.

He told them to check their weapons, clean them and make damn sure they wouldn't misfire or jam, and be ready to ride out of town at dawn.

His plan was to hit Willy Boy and his bunch in the Larned Hotel before they even knew he was in town. Hit them and kill them if need be. There was only one hotel in Larned, and if they were still in town they would be there. They had been running hard, had one man shot up and should be ready for the rest.

Handshoe thought about it as he lay on his bed trying to sleep. Evidently they had contact with Conover and wounded but did not capture him. Why not? Six against one. He'd find out. By now Conover should be dead.

There had been a time or two in the past when Handshoe himself had plans for killing the man.

Morning dawned chilly and cloudy. Handshoe and his men rode with the first light without breakfast. He told them they could eat like pigs when they bagged the six men. Each of his bounty hunters had been promised a $20 bonus for each of the Willy Boy Gang captured or killed.

He was putting ten percent of the total price on the line for the men and they appreciated it. They all would try that much harder to earn an extra half year's pay in one deadly morning.

Handshoe and his men rode into town in pairs before seven-thirty that morning.

He went into the hotel and checked the register. None of the names of the Willy Boy Gang showed. But Handshoe knew they had a habit of using different names each time they registered in a hotel. He talked to the desk clerk who had been there the afternoon before.

"Yeah, six guys registered. In fact ten registered."

"Did some of them show up in pairs?"

"Yeah, men come in that way all the time. Safer to travel that way. Fact is, all ten were in pairs."

Handshoe took a $20 gold piece out of his pocket and flipped it. The room clerk watched it with fascination.

"I've got a letter that describes six men I'm hunting. They're all wanted men. If you can tell me that they're here, and which rooms they have, you get the double eagle."

The clerk read the letter slowly. He nodded, then looked at his register.

"Can't be sure which are which, but all six of them came in in a row. I've got a system for assigning rooms. The six of them are in rooms twenty-two and twenty-four, twenty-seven and twenty-eight, and twenty-nine and thirty. All on the second floor."

"You seen any of them this morning?" Handshoe asked.

"Don't remember any of them. You might check the dining room."

Handshoe flipped the coin and let it come down toward the room clerk who grabbed it.

"You check the dining room and I'll watch for them to come down the stairs."

Handshoe designated four men to watch the stairs with the desk clerk. They sat in shabby furniture, reading newspapers or magazines.

Handshoe took five men with him and stared past the door to the dining room. He saw Gunner Johnson at once. He was too big to be missed. A careful study of the other people in the eatery showed that none of the other Willy Boy Gang was there. Handshoe walked into the dining room with four of his men and started to take the table beside Gunner.

Handshoe bumped Gunner's chair. When Gunner looked around, Handshoe excused himself. That was the signal. One of the men with him grabbed Gunner's six-gun and pulled it from his holster. Handshoe put his revolver's muzzle under Gunner's chin before he could react.

"Gunner Johnson, you're under arrest for murder. You give me any problems and I'll shoot you dead right here, you understand?"

Gunner looked at them and relaxed and the men beside him grabbed his arms and lifted him out of the chair. As soon as Gunner stood, Handshoe started to move the six-gun to Gunner's side.

Gunner exploded, ramming one elbow back into the man behind him, breaking a rib and pushing the broken end into his lung. The man fell on the floor gasping for breath.

The second man he punched in the face with his big fist, knocked out three teeth and slammed him over the table of a couple who was in the middle of breakfast.

The woman who was knocked off her chair screamed, and screamed, and wouldn't stop. Her husband helped her up and they hurried toward the only exit, the woman screaming and crying and yelling at the top of her voice all the way.

Two more men rushed up. Handshoe had been jolted aside by the men trying to help him. He had no shot. Gunner spun around, kicked the third man in the leg, then pounding him with his fists, ducking and coming back to the standing man on the other side. From behind Gunner, one of the bounty hunters slammed his gun butt into Gunner's kidney. He gasped in pain.

With the momentary calm, Handshoe jumped forward and crashed the butt of his big .45 down on Gunner's head and he went down in a wild flailing of out of control arms and legs. They had to carry him out of the dining room. But first they tied his hands together behind his back and tied his feet with rawhide. When he came to, he bellowed in alarm and surprise. Quickly they put a gag around his mouth and the four of them carried him out of the dining room.

Handshoe talked with the room clerk a minute, handed him a ten dollar bill and they put Gunner in a small room just off the lobby. The clerk locked the door and kept the key.

187

Handshoe pointed upstairs and all of them except the man with the punctured lung moved up the steps as quietly as they could.

The first door they came to that they wanted was 22. Handshoe kept three men there with him and sent one man down the hall to cover the other five doors. He had told them they would kick in the doors all together. Shoot first and worry about it later.

Handshoe raised his hand and brought it down. The biggest man with him kicked open the door and headed inside the room. A second man shouldered in behind him. Suddenly a shotgun blast ripped into both men and dumped them in the hall where they fell, now only a dead mass of flesh and bone.

Down the hall the other doors jolted open under the boots but the Handshoe men came out quickly. No one was in any of the other rooms.

Handshoe cowered in the hallway. He motioned his men to come toward him but they remained where they were. He bellowed in fear when a double barreled shotgun poked around the corner of the door.

A moment later it blasted and the third

man he had with him was almost cut in half by the 10 gauge load of double-ought buck balls. Handshoe ran down the hall to the steps and vanished. The other six men on Handshoe's payroll stayed in the rooms they had kicked open not wanting to make themselves targets.

In room 22, Willy Boy looked down the hall from his room and then stepped quickly to the window as he reloaded the sawed off shotgun that hung by a cord around his neck. He had already opened the window. Now he slid out, hung by his hands, dropped the six feet to the alley and ran down where the rest of his men waited on their horses. Only Gunner was missing.

"They got Gunner but we didn't have time to get him out," the Professor said. "Little shithead of a clerk locked him in a room off the lobby."

"We know which horses are theirs?" Willy Boy asked.

"Not a chance," Eagle said. "Probably 30 horses on that block."

"Come on then, let's ride. We want to leave a plain trail out of town so Handshoe will follow it. I don't know how many men he's got, but it's three less than it was ten minutes ago."

Juan rode up and frowned. "We just

leaving Gunner back there?"

"For now. First we have to take care of Handshoe. If we can pick him off, there goes the paycheck for the others and they'll scatter like flies off a kicked horse turd."

They rode down Main Street and at the end of it fired off half a dozen pistol shots harmlessly as if someone was after them. By the time they were out of sight, at least 50 people were in the street watching them ride off toward the Arkansas River.

# Chapter Fifteen

Michael Handshoe came out of the small room off the lobby with his six-gun up and ready. He saw none of the Willy Boy Gang and looked at the desk clerk.

"They're all gone," the hotel man said with undisguised disdain. "You're safe now."

"They shotgunned my men, killed three or four upstairs. You better send for the sheriff. I've got to get the rest of my men." He went up the steps fearfully, stepped over the bodies of his dead men and snarled at the empty hallway.

"You cowards can come out now, the bad man has gone away."

Heads poked out of doors and soon he had all six men. They stared at the three corpses still sprawled on the floor. Gingerly they picked their way over and around the bodies on their way to the stairs.

"Damn, three of them," one of the men said. "No way you can go up against a shotgun with a pistol."

Handshoe pretended not to hear him. Downstairs they found the sheriff there waiting. He talked to Handshoe a moment, then took two deputies and hurried up the steps.

Outside, they looked at their leader. "Let's get after them. Spread out and find out which way they went. I thought I heard some shooting, so it shouldn't be hard. Let's mount up first and be ready to ride."

Fifteen minutes later they were on the trail of the six men heading out of town to the west. "Back the way they came?" Handshoe asked the man beside him. "Why would they want to turn back this way?"

The man knew better than to answer an angry Handshoe. They rode hard. Their tracker, still among the living, led the way. Soon the trail curved and then headed back toward town south of the place and charged straight ahead for the woods along the Arkansas River.

Handshoe held up his hand and the men stopped. He stared at the brush. "Could be a trap," he said.

He had stopped 300 yards from the river and now scowled. He knew the men were watching him. They had to either storm into the brush or turn around and ride away from it. One or the other.

"Goddamn!" he snorted and kicked his mount in the sides and galloped straight ahead. It was a tough 30 seconds for the men. But soon they knew there was no trap hiding in the brush and no sudden eruption of rifle and shotgun fire.

The tracker took back the lead and found the trail working along the river. After a quarter of a mile downstream, the tracker, a southerner named Al Jacoby stopped and looked at Handshoe.

"I don't like it, sir. They're leading us right where they want us to go. They could have an ambush anywhere along here and cut us to pieces."

Handshoe came up and glared at the man. "You don't get paid to think or to like, Jacoby. Get back to tracking. I make the decisions around here."

Jacoby stared at him a minute, then rode up closer. "That's damn fine with me, Handshoe. You make all the decisions you want to. First, you give me my three days pay. I'm riding out of here."

Handshoe sputtered a minute, then dug in his pocket for a ten dollar gold piece. "Three dollars a day, like I promised. Now get out of here."

The five hired men watched Jacoby go.

"Any other cowards want to leave a good paying job?" Handshoe asked.

Nobody moved. He took the lead and followed the easy to read trail another mile along the banks of the river.

Every step now, Handshoe wondered the same thing the tracker had. Why were the outlaws leading them this way with no real try at breaking out to escape? Were they simply luring them into a trap they knew about? Unlikely. None of the men were from this area.

Time. Were they stretching out the chase for some reason to gain time?

At least he captured one of them. He would make back his expenses and a small profit. He wanted more. Handshoe picked up the pace and moved along the plain trail faster.

Now the brush along the river thinned to a few cottonwoods and some tall hickory. There was very little cover here and the men shifted in their saddles knowing they could be under the sights of five rifles.

Abruptly the trail angled to the west, away from the river and toward a small rise of ground. It wasn't more than 50 feet high, but in the flatlands of Kansas it was a mountain. It was rocky and the soil thin, so only a few tufts of grass grew there and no trees or brush at all.

Handshoe watched the skyline of the little hill as the trail wound that way, then swung around it and he could see where the outlaws' horses had picked up speed and galloped back toward the woods less than a quarter of a mile away.

The first rifle shot from the woods took the bounty hunters by surprise when they were only 50 yards from the brushy section of the Arkansas River.

The Professor held his mount's muzzle as the bounty hunters moved by cautiously through the brush less than 30 yards away. He had turned off the trail the others had left and hidden in the thick cover less than a quarter of a mile downstream after they first gained the river.

When the posse was well past, the Professor mounted and walked his horse back toward town. When he was sure the searchers were well hidden in the brush, he galloped for a quarter of a mile, then let his big bay lope along into town.

The Professor found where they had left Gunner's horse and moved him down toward the hotel and tied him beside his own. Then he adjusted his black hat, wiped some of the dust off his face from the ride, and walked up the steps into the hotel.

There was no sign of the sheriff. The lawman had probably taken the bodies away and left.

The Professor walked into the front door and up to the room clerk drawing his six-gun smoothly and pushing the muzzle under the man's chin. "Where did the bounty hunter leave Gunner?" the Professor demanded quietly.

"Don't shoot!" the room clerk said. Sweat beaded his forehead. His eyes were wild. For a moment, the Professor thought he might faint.

"Over here, right over here in the conference room," he said. "Mr. Handshoe said I should leave him there. But I'll be glad to open the door for you."

No one else was in the small lobby right then. The Professor pulled down the gun but kept it touching the man's side as they walked to the door where Gunner had been left. The clerk unlocked the panel and opened it.

He tried to step back, but the Professor pushed him inside and closed the door. The window shade was drawn.

"Lift the shade," the Professor said. "Get some light in here."

With the light they could see Gunner laying on the floor tied hand and foot.

"Cut him loose," the Professor ordered.

The small clerk took out a pen knife from his pocket and sawed the rawhide strips in half. The Professor untied the cloth that served as a gag, and saw that Gunner was conscious.

"Hey, big man, how do you feel?"

"Stupid for getting captured. There was only five of them."

"Forget it, we've got them on the run." The Professor saw the bloody scrape on Gunner's head. "Looks like you got pounded on the head."

"Yeah, hurts, but I can ride. We out of town?"

"Sure are, and so is Handshoe, the bounty hunter."

The clerk stood against the wall watching. The Professor took Gunner's arm and helped him stand. He was dizzy at first but that passed. Then they walked around the room half a dozen times, until Gunner was steady on his feet.

The Professor looked at Gunner. "Where's your hat?"

"Left it in my room."

The Professor looked at the clerk. "We're going in the lobby. You get a hat for

Gunner. One somebody left here or your own, I don't care. Make it a hat and damn fast, otherwise you'll be dead before dinner."

"Yes . . . yes sir. Mine's under the front desk."

They went out. The clerk handed his brown low crowned hat to Gunner who put it on. It was slightly small but fit well enough. They walked outside and directly to their horses.

For a minute, the Professor thought Gunner was going to need help to mount. That would attract attention. He made two tries and then swung his leg over and hit leather.

They rode out of town to the east slowly, then when they came to the last house lifted the pace into a lope and covered the ground to the river side.

"Everyone else all right?" Gunner asked.

"All healthy," the Professor said. "We heard the woman scream downstairs evidently when they had the fight with you. Eagle had been out for a walk and he saw it through the window and came up the back stairs and warned us.

"We all went out our windows into the alley and got ready to ride. Willy Boy waited for them with his sawed off shotgun and cut down three of them before they all ran and hid. Then he went out the window and here we are."

"Thanks for coming back for me," Gunner said. "We riding or going to fight them?"

"Willy Boy is tired of running. We'll try to discourage the bounty hunter anyway that we can."

Gunner was watching the trail along the river.

"Lots of hoof prints along here."

The Professor grinned. "Indeed there are, young man. Five of our people, and seven or eight of that bounty hunter after us. When we catch up to them, or maybe before, Willy Boy is going to hit them with the rifles. If we're close enough we'll get them in a cross fire from the rear."

Gunner grinned. "I like that. They hurt me."

Gunner and the Professor rode for another five minutes before they heard gunfire ahead of them. Then they galloped.

They came through the brush and saw the bounty hunter men diving off their horses and looking for cover. Three of the mounted men tried to ride out, but their horses were shot out from under them.

Two of the grounded men lifted their hands in surrender and stood. One of them was shot in the back and driven forward. The other one dropped to the ground quickly.

"Which one is the leader?" the Professor asked Gunner.

They had pulled up in brush along the river and could see the fighting.

"The one with the white horse. Big guy."

The Professor had pulled his rifle and sat on his sturdy horse. He took careful aim. His first shot missed, but he levered in a second round and knocked the man off the white horse.

Two of the bounty hunters lifted up and ran back the way they had come toward a shallow ditch that put them out of sight.

Two more stood with hands over their heads and the firing from the heavy brush stopped.

"Get the hell out of here and never work for a bounty hunter again!" Willy Boy's surprisingly strong voice boomed at them.

Another man stood slowly from behind a horse and holding his right arm, hurried back toward the ditch.

The Professor grinned. "Let's go see how the boys did," he said and they rode downstream toward the other fighters.

Willy Boy laughed and hugged the big man when Gunner jumped down from his horse.

"Gunner, you old reprobate! Damn glad to see you. Knew they couldn't keep a good man like you down. Welcome back!"

Gunner blinked back moisture in his eyes, then shook hands with the rest of the gang and sat down suddenly. "I thought I was dead back there. They tied me up. They hit me hard with their gun butts. It really hurts."

"You're back with us now, Gunner. We take care of our own. And we just cut up that Handshoe bunch so he won't ever bother us again."

"I got Handshoe," the Professor said. "Gunner told me which one he was and I blasted him right out of his saddle."

"Good, without a leader that should end it," Willy Boy said. "Now, let's get downstream aways and set up camp and cook some beans. Damn but I'm hungry for some good camp cooked baked beans."

They rode. At three that afternoon they found a spot to camp and built a fire and set things up. This time they let the beans boil over the continuous fire. They lay back on their blankets and watched the birds in the trees.

"What's next?" the Professor asked. "Where do we go from here?"

"Been thinking on that," Willy Boy said. "Hell, we're free men. We're not under any threat of a hangman's noose or a long jail stretch. That's fine, but not enough. We now need a mission, something to keep busy at. I'm still looking for Deeds Conover. But he's hurt and won't surface for a time. I was thinking about heading up to Idaho, or down to Mexico. Gunner, anything that you want to do right now?"

"No, just stay with you. Help you, Willy Boy. That's all."

"Professor? How about you?"

"There's this little blonde lady down in Memphis that is really something to see. I'd just as soon head that way if we're taking a vote. But now, if you're talking business, there is something else. I nearly got killed up in Colorado at a little town that has a damn rich bank and good protection. I'd give half a year's pay to go up there with some stalwart companions and dismantle every safeguard they put on their little bank, and rob them right out of existence!"

"Yeah, now that does sound like a possible target, and one we all could benefit from. Let's see what else we have on the auction block. Johnny Joe? Where were you headed before you got kicked into the calaboose?"

"Big poker game out in San Francisco. I played in it once, and the man who beat me cheated and I never could figure out how. Now I know. I learned every way possible to cheat in poker so I can catch the damn cheaters. Now I'd give a whole lot to be in San Francisco and tangle with Francis X. Delany. The old bastard must be in his sixties by now."

"Interesting, but hell, we don't need to decide right now," Willy Boy said. "We got some time. We still have enough money. All we have to do is relax for a week or so, slip into some town and live the good life until we run out of funds. Then we'll look to our banker and good friend, the Professor, to help us resupply our pocketbooks."

Everyone laughed.

Willy Boy looked over at Juan who was stirring the beans and adding water. "Juan, when the hell those beans going to be ready?"

# Chapter Sixteen

The last figure to lift up from behind a horse and move with the consent of the outlaws back out of range, limped on a bruised right leg, and tenderly held his left arm. A bullet had shattered his shoulder and the pain was debilitating. He struggled to the ditch and slumped there, looking at the other men.

Two more had been killed. How many wounded? Suddenly he didn't want to know. He just wanted vengeance.

Michael Handshoe pushed his hand into the front of his shirt to support his arm while he fashioned a sling from his neckerchief. Pain clouded his mind as he worked. Everything took three times as long.

First he had to decide what to do, consciously. Then he had to order his arm to move. At last he had the wounded left arm firmly in place. His revolver had remained in his holster when he had been shot out of his saddle.

In ten years of chasing outlaws he had never been shot before. First time for everything, he decided. Except dying. That was a one time affair.

He saw two of his men run to catch horses. He had no idea where his was. Handshoe called to one of the men to bring him a horse, but the man shrugged, grabbed the nearest mount and rode away, back toward town.

Two more men left the ditch, walking toward town. Three horses were dead. Two had been ridden off. There had to be some more around, but he couldn't see them. He probably couldn't catch one if he found it.

One of the new men rode up and looked at Handshoe.

"I'm leaving, too. You didn't say this was gonna be an all out war. Hell, I was in one of them once. Didn't like it." He turned and rode away.

Handshoe tried to call after him, but the man quickly rode out of sight. The bounty hunter sat up and looked around. No more horses, no men to help him.

"Goddamn, I'm gonna get him, or get some of them. Damn them!"

He struggled to his feet and stumbled for the first few steps. Then he got his balance and stared ahead at the brushline and walked toward it. They would bed down before long. He could track them and when they were sleeping he would slip up and knife the whole crew!

The fantasy kept him moving. At the brush he went through to the river and cupped his hand and lifted water to his mouth. When he had his fill he washed some of the blood off his arm. He figured the bleeding had stopped on his shoulder. If it didn't he'd die from loss of blood in two hours.

He found the tracks of the outlaws' horses and started following them. It might take him all night but he would find them.

He figured it was only a little after midday; no, before that. They had hit the hotel at about 7:30, that couldn't have been more than two hours ago. Lots of time before dark. Now if the outlaws only felt safe and stopped early to do some cooking or just resting.

Handshoe kept walking. Twice he fell and the jolting of his shoulder brought a cry of pain from him. He struggled up, found a stick to use as a walking cane, and moved on. The prints showed that the outlaws were not riding fast. They were walking their mounts, moving away from the engagement. Sure of their safety.

His grin turned into a hatred-smile as he dreamed what he would do to the bastards.

It was a little after five o'clock that afternoon when he smelled the smoke. He was downwind of them. Yes! They had stopped just as he figured they would. He had learned a lot about the outlaw mind after chasing so many for so long.

Handshoe worked downstream carefully, making sure of his steps now, watching for any sign of the camp ahead. He took detours around open spots along the river bank to stay in his cover. Twice he sat down and rested.

He checked his revolver and pushed in a sixth round. He had his favorite 1860 army percussion revolver that he had converted to solid cartridges. He loved the eight-inch barrel. Made it much more accurate than the four or six-inch models. Of course, it was not a fast draw weapon.

He felt on his gunbelt and found all the loops full. He had twenty more rounds. Good. He moved again.

It was still broad daylight when he had his first glimpse of the camp. It was in an open spot by the river near a sandy shore line. They had built a cooking fire, and rolled out their blankets already. He could see three of them.

He was surprised to find Gunner Johnson there. The bastards! They had sent a man circling back to the hotel to rescue his prisoner! He hated to be out-thought as well as out-gunned. It firmed his resolve even more. He knew he would be no match for them in a shootout. Not at five to one and he with only a revolver. But come night he could move in and use his knife. Yes, the knife.

Another three hours and it would be dark. Then he would work his will on them. As many as he could. If one screamed or made too much noise, he would slip away in the darkness. Not even the Indian could track him in the middle of the night.

Horse! Yes, he would steal one of their horses and have him set at a particular spot where he would retreat to. Then he'd be away and riding for town. He'd report this new outrage to the sheriff.

He couldn't remember it ever getting dark so slowly. Handshoe had moved up on the camp. Now he was in brush 30 yards away from the closest man. He could hear snatches of their talks. They did lots of laughing. None of them seemed injured or wounded. That would change damn fast!

Handshoe felt wetness on his arm. He looked at his shoulder. It was bleeding again. There was a small pool of blood below his elbow where the red stuff had dripped onto the ground. He stared at it for a minute before he realized he had to do something about it. He was bleeding to death.

He could run into their camp and ask the outlaws to bind up his shoulder and save his life. Handshoe snorted. Not a chance in hell he would do that.

He could move closer and open fire and shoot it out with them from behind good cover. He should be able to get three or four of them, maybe enough so they wouldn't follow him. Then he could steal a horse and get back to the doctor at Larned.

Maybe. Hell, it was his best option.

*He wanted to hurt them bad, make them regret they tangled with him.*

A wave of dizziness hit him and Handshoe had to lean against a walnut tree to keep his balance. When the spell passed, he set his jaw grimly. He had no option. If he waited any longer he could pass out. He leaned forward and began crawling forward using one hand.

Yes! It wasn't as hard as he thought it might be. Once he felt a black cloud drop over him and he sighed and fell on his stomach on the soft mulch of the brush-line. He came to quickly and shook his head. He had seen a log just ahead. It looked like a hickory tree that had dropped years ago, but would absorb a lot of pistol and rifle fire. It was two feet thick and offered him a good firing point.

He got to it and saw he was only 20 yards from the camp, and the brush had thinned here, so he could count on most of his shots running true without skipping off branches and small trees.

He sat a moment resting, then Hand-shoe took out his old Colt and thumbed back the hammer pressing it against his chest to soften the click.

He rested the long barrel on the log and picked out a target. Willy Boy was to one side behind one of the other men. He saw the small Mexican working over the fire. Best target. He leveled in the six-gun and sighted at the Mexican's chest.

Sweat beaded his forehead. Michael Handshoe paused for just a moment, then he firmed his jaw and squeezed the trigger. Handshoe didn't see where the round hit. Quickly he thumbed back the hammer, aimed at another man and fired. He got off four shots before any return fire came. Then the blue smoke gave away his position.

He ducked as the first rain of lead came from the outlaws. When it paused, he lifted up and fired twice more. Then he pushed out the casings and loaded six more rounds. It was harder than he thought. He had never reloaded with just one hand before.

Now rifle fire peppered the log. He wanted to move but he wasn't sure he could. Handshoe lifted up and fired again. This time he had no target, just into the area around the campfire. They all had found something to hide behind.

He cocked the hammer again and looked for a target. A bullet hit him in his right shoulder, slamming him backward. He lost the six-gun. The pain was unbearable. He screeched in agony, then bit off the sound and found his weapon. He cocked it and pushed it over the log and fired, not looking at the camp.

He fired all six rounds and tried to reload. His right hand didn't do exactly what he wanted it to do. He pushed out the rounds and fumbled for new ones.

Rounds kept zapping over the top of the log as he lay behind it reloading. He pushed his revolver over the log without lifting up and squeezed the trigger. Then he brought it down, cocked it and pushed it over the log again. Three rifle rounds blasted and one of them hit the 1860 converted army percussion revolver, spun it out of his hand and broke two of his fingers.

Part of the splattering lead bullet came off the weapon and slanted downward and tore through his right cheek and out the other cheek missing his teeth and tongue.

"We got him," a voice called.

"Not him, I think we ruined his six-gun and probably his hand at the same time."

"I'll look," Eagle said.

Handshoe wasn't aware of any sounds of movements before he looked up from where he lay behind the log and found the Comanche staring down at him.

"His stinger is pulled," Eagle said.

The others came then. The Mexican stepped up and kicked him in the stomach. Handshoe vomited to one side, then he saw that Juan Romero had a bloody mark on his upper arm.

"At least I got one of you," Handshoe said. "You going to tie up my shoulders and stop the blood, or let me lay here and bleed to death?"

Willy Boy stared down at him. "I should put a bullet through your brain, but that would be too fast. You've caused us a lot of trouble, Handshoe."

"Yeah, but not as much as you caused me."

Gunner came up limping, holding his left leg.

"You're a bad man," Gunner said.

He let go of his leg, drew his revolver and shot Handshoe in the thigh. Nobody moved to stop Gunner. None of the outlaws said a word.

"Now you know what it feels like to be shot in the leg," Gunner said. He turned and hobbled back to the fire.

"Why do you do this, Handshoe?" Willy Boy asked. "Why hunt down men for profit?"

"I used to be a lawman. I starved and my wife left me. A judge asked me to bring in a man, so I did. He paid me the $500 reward. I worked for him for three years. Now I'm on my own. I make over $5,000 a year."

Handshoe screeched in pain and his eyes closed. When they opened he could only whisper. "Finish it for me. Just one round."

None of the outlaws offered to kill him.

"Then give me a gun and let me do it. One round in a gun and get out of sight. Sometimes a man likes a little peace and privacy when he dies."

Nobody provided him with a weapon.

He looked up at Willy Boy. "Damn you all. Damn you to hell!"

"That's a sure bet, Handshoe," Johnny Joe said. "You'll be there to welcome us. Only difference is you'll be there today. None of us has any plans on seeing you for a lot of long years yet. So you just roast in hell by yourself till then."

The Willy Boy Gang members drifted back to the fire. Juan had his shoulder bandaged up, then he worked on Gunner's leg. Soon the only one left beside Handshoe was the Professor.

"You want to die alone?" the Professor asked.

"No, damnit no."

"Talk about home, family. I've heard that makes it easier."

"Why?"

"Why not. I don't know much about death and dying. Church people say there's a life after death. I never really believed that. Where is it? The body is still here rotting in a grave. Doesn't make much logical sense. I'm afraid that this is it. This is the only life we'll ever know."

"You a philosopher?" Handshoe asked. "I never would have thought it." Then he nodded. "Oh, yeah, the Professor, the one who went to college and taught school."

"True. How did you find us so fast?"

"Wrote a letter to Texas. Sheriff down there wants you bad. He sent descriptions, habits, crimes, everything they knew about each one of you."

"Must have helped."

"Did. Then you kept asking about Deeds Conover. That was like a sign post that moved us along."

"Won't make that mistake again." The Professor took out his six-gun and pushed the rounds out of it. He pocketed all but one and held up the weapon.

"You still want one round, Handshoe?" the Professor asked.

"Damned right. I'm hurting too much."

"You got it. One revolver, and one loose round. Can you load it."

Handshoe nodded. The Professor put the weapon in his hand and gave him the .45 round. Then he walked away from the bounty hunter and stepped behind the solid trunk of a big cottonwood.

"I gave him one round," the Professor said. "Might find some cover, you guys. He's loading the round."

The other five men scurried behind cover.

A moment later the sound of a revolver

shot blasted through the quietness of the Kansas plains.

The Professor hurried up to the log. The muzzle of the gun was still in Handshoe's mouth. A four-inch wide chunk of his skull had been blasted into the brush.

Willy Boy looked down at the bounty hunter and nodded. "That's that," he said and turned away.

# Chapter Seventeen

*After Handshoe* killed himself, Willy Boy and his men packed up and rode another ten miles down the river to a new camp spot and put the beans back on to finish cooking.

They all lounged around the campfire, even though it was nearly ten o'clock. Nobody wanted to turn in. Nobody wanted to talk much.

"Thank God nobody has a harmonica," Willy Boy said, and everyone laughed. They had eaten beans and bacon for an hour and pronounced the mix delicious. There was still enough for breakfast.

"In the morning we float into the nearest town, register at a hotel one at a time over a couple of hours, and rest up and relax and get those gunshots all looked at. We've got three now."

They all nodded.

"Then we work hard at having a good time for a week. At the end of that time we'll be riding out. Not just sure where yet, but we'll head out and see if we can take care of one of your problems."

Willy Boy stopped talking then, pushed sticks into the fire and watched them burn.

Juan Romero had been thinking about his wife Juanita and their year old baby, Ernesto. She would be at her mother's house in Guadalupe waiting for him. There was no way he could explain how desperately he wanted to be home, to see Juanita, to touch her, to watch her dancing dark eyes and the wonderful smile she kept just for him.

But he was here now. He had made a bargain, and even if it might have been a bargain with a small sized devil, he would honor it and do as he had agreed. If it was not for Willy Boy, right now Juan knew he would be in a prison somewhere, serving the 20 years the judge had warned him about.

A month, six months, even a year of riding with Willy Boy and his debt would be paid. The gang would have done what it set out to do, to stay alive, and to try to right some of the wrongs that had been done to its members.

The gunshot he had suffered today was not that serious. A flesh wound on his left arm. He had bound it up and knew it would be painful for two weeks, then it would heal and leave a scar but nothing more serious. The revolver round had cut a swath through his outer arm but missed the bone and the lead was gone. He was not concerned about it.

Yes, he understood that now he was a wanted man in *Los Estados Unidos*. Wanted dead or alive. He did not have a guilty conscience. He had been defending himself. Anyway, once he was across the international boundary into Mexico he would be safe, and he could spend the rest of his days in his native land and learn to put up with its problems and petty officials and the military dictators who came and went.

He had held such high hopes for the new land. But he found that dishonest and self serving officials were not limited to Mexico. Until he could return he would ride with the *muchacho loco*.

He would do what he had to do, whether it was against the law or not. He was no longer interested in the law of this country. Soon he would be gone and back to his family.

He remembered the sweet soft way Juanita came to him in the night as they lay in their bed. She was so delightful, so beautiful, and so needing him.

Sometimes they made love all night and the next morning he would get up too tired and groggy to go to work. She would call him *El Toro,* and he would laugh and she would tease him, and soon he was ready to go to work.

Juan did not dare think of their small son Ernesto, almost a year old now. If he thought about the sweet, small boy, all giggles and bright brown eyes and tottering around with his first steps, Juan knew that he just might slip away in the night and ride like the wind without stopping all the way to Mexico.

Juan stared at the fire, and saw Juanita there nodding and telling him that he was doing the right thing. Six months now or even a year, was better than forever in a *gringo* prison.

Juan remembered Juanita's beautiful face as he pulled his blankets up and pushed his feet toward the fire.

Johnny Joe watched the fire for a time, then stretched out and looked upward through the leaves at the stars. There were a million of them out tonight and there wasn't a cloud in the Kansas sky to hide them. He found the big dipper and the little dipper, and then the stars began to look like the Mississippi River gambling stern wheelers and side wheelers.

Someday he would get back to them.

Right now he had bought into this game and he was determined to stay in the game until the final pot was awarded. It might help him get to San Francisco. He shook his head. Getting to the big town was no problem.

For $200 he could buy a ticket to San Francisco. His problem was getting enough cold, hard cash ready to get into the game with Francis X. Delany. It would take $1000 for his weekly game.

Johnny Joe would need $10,000 at least, to go up against Delany in his big Christmas Poker Spectacular. In it each man put up the ante, from $10,000 to $30,000 and they played until one man owned all of the money. The game was usually limited to 12 players.

Not just any 12, but men of some reputation. Honest men who wouldn't cheat, and — since Delany had final say on who got to play — men Delany thought he could whip.

Getting there was only a minor part of the story. But if they could loot a bank or two, and he could pick up some small change at neighborhood saloons, he might have enough to make a stab at it. Might.

For this he needed the Professor. Not necessarily the rest of the gang, but the

Professor would be the key. When the right time came he would make a pitch to the Professor. They would go fifty-fifty partners with the chance of earning a return of ten-to-one on their money.

When they went into town the next day, Johnny Joe would spend his time gambling. He still had most of the $400 they had split after the bank. If he could boost that up to $1,000 over the next week, he would have the start of his entry fee.

Now he could think of little else down the road but San Francisco. He was in this game until the last card was played, or some smart bounty hunter broke up the game with the ace of spades, the death card.

For Johnny Joe there was no going home. His father had fought in the big war for the south, and as a result lost his small plantation and all of his buildings and animals. A Yankee patrol had burned it to the ground when one of the darkies had taken a shot at the dreaded Bluebellies.

His father had been killed in the war, his mother fled from the house after they started burning it down and he lost track of her. He couldn't go home.

That's when he realized that he no longer had a derringer. Any gambler worth his fancy vest had to have a hideout gun. He would invest in one as soon as he found a gunshop that had one to his liking. He preferred the .22 caliber size. It was highly effective and bluffed as good as a .45. The .22 caliber derringer was one-third the size of the larger weapon and could be carried in a variety of locations.

Johnny Joe Williams toyed with just where to carry his new weapon. He could have a tailor sew a special pocket in his vest for it, so it lay inside his jacket and on the outside of the vest.

Or should he carry it lower? He stared at the stars again, saw one turn from red to blue and back to red again, and decided it was time he went to sleep.

Gunner Johnson sat up as long as Willy Boy did, then when their leader lay down, so did Gunner. He turned on his side so he could see Willy Boy but didn't know if he was sleeping or not.

Gunner felt the wound in his leg. It hurt all the time now. The bullet had gone all the way through his left thigh. It hurt to walk, but he wouldn't let on. He had to help protect Willy Boy.

The big man scowled at the sky. He didn't see why people were always trying to hurt them. They were just trying to mind their own business. Course they did have to find that bad bounty hunter who killed Willy Boy's pa. That they had to do. Maybe they would find him soon.

Gunner thought back over the past two or three weeks and he couldn't remember a time when he had been any happier. He was riding with Willy Boy and he felt important. He had a job to do and he could do it.

He frowned as he watched Willy Boy sleeping soundly now. He wasn't exactly sure what his job was, but he always helped. He found wood and got the horses and put out the fire. In town he watched Willy Boy and walked near him and frowned at anybody who looked mean at Willy Boy.

Yes, sir, just about the best job he'd ever had. He didn't care if it ever ended. Out here in the country, or in town with Willy Boy, it was all fine with him. He sat up, looked around camp, but everyone seemed settled down, so he lay back down, closed his eyes and went to sleep almost at once.

The Professor had seen Gunner sit up. He almost said something but the big man laid back down.

The Professor had been trying to figure out just what he should do. They were away free and clear. He could tell Willy Boy that he had done his duty to the group, served his time helping them and now they all were out into the brave new world.

He could tell Willy Boy that he really didn't want to be a part of the gang. If he did he would form his own, maybe three of them, including one woman, and they would specialize in doing banks and riding the train between jobs and staying in fancy hotels.

He didn't really like living off the back of a horse and sleeping on the ground. It was fine if he had to ride away from a posse or an angry bank owner, but for the most part he would rather play the part of a city slicker bank robber.

Still, the West was his best territory. What little law there was came up short or ineffective. The banks themselves were simple to rob and escape, without a lot of fancy safety devices and guards and alarms and shotguns in drawers.

He turned over, not ready to go to sleep. Still, if the bunch would help him turn that Colorado bank inside out, he would really be delighted. It would take at least five men to rob that one. It wouldn't be a closing time job. It would be a high noon affair with shotguns pumping out lead and windows crashing and get away horses out behind the bank.

All of that, five men and a lot of luck, and they could get away with $20,000 cash. He grinned. Now that was a figure that he could appreciate.

He turned over again. Hell, he wasn't sure what to do. He'd lay around the next town, case the bank, play a little, find out the quality of the ladies of the evening, and see if there was an unhappy wife he could make smile again.

Then when Willy Boy decided what was next on the agenda for the gang, he'd figure out if he wanted to go along with it or cut out on his own again.

That determined, the Professor winked at the north star and promptly went to sleep.

Eagle had been sleeping once. Something awoke him. He didn't move but his senses came alert and he watched what he could see from where he lay on his side. He could scan about half of the camp and see three of the sleeping men.

The noise came again, a thin ripping sound. He sat up cautiously, his hand closing around his six-gun. The sound was near the spot where the food sat in the gunny sacks.

A glimmer of moonlight slanted through wavering leaves and he saw the culprit. A squirrel jumped out of the burlap sack after chewing a hole in it. The squirrel had been tearing open one of the paper sacks, probably one that held dried fruit.

Eagle wondered about Idaho. He wanted more than anything to get to Boise and look over the Fourteenth. There would be men in the unit that had been there the night his father and his family died. One trooper told him that most men spent their whole 20 years in the same regiment.

He would not rest until he had avenged his family's death. It was his duty as a Comanche. Even if he was part white eye now, he still had deep feelings and beliefs rooted in the Comanche culture.

A warrior did not walk away from a wounded friend. A warrior did not let the death of a friend go unpunished. He must punish those who cut down his family even after they all had surrendered.

He lay down again and let the anger flow out of him. He cleansed his spirit, he let the positive powers renew his strength. He purified himself.

A moment later he saw a night hawk slanting through the sky blotting out the stars on its trek. The lowly night hawk could make the heavens change!

Willy Boy. The kid was a terror. He knew what he wanted and he would get it. He would eventually catch Deeds Conover and torture him to death. But the young man was also vicious and cruel and seemed to like to see men suffer. That, Eagle did not approve of.

A battle was a battle. Warriors fought like warriors, but most of life was not a battle. Willy Boy was always at war with everyone.

He had to get to Boise. He still had almost all the $400 from the bank robbery. That would be plenty to get to the railroad and buy a ticket to Idaho or as close as he could come. He could find Boise.

Had he paid his debt to Willy Boy yet? Had he paid him back for saving him from a hangman's noose or a quicker death in prison? He would know soon.

Willy Boy had not gone to sleep yet. He had seen Gunner watching him. A few kindnesses in the jail cell and the man had become his slave for life.

Willy Boy thought back over the last two weeks. Much had happened. They had broken out, they had hung together and defeated the best that the law and bounty hunters could throw against them.

Was it over? Was this phase of the Willy Boy Gang through? Or did they go to settle with the needs of other members, and rob banks and trains and stage coaches as a profession? It was something to think about.

A trip to Idaho, a stop in Colorado, a run to Mexico to leave Juan, and along the way, the Professor leading them to the best banks to rob. Maybe even a trip all the way to San Francisco to help Johnny Joe.

It was so tempting. Deeds Conover was still out there, alive and breathing. He had to be put under the sod. But Willy Boy knew he had taken a good swing at the man. They had hurt him and sent him running. Now perhaps it was time to look at the other members of their little band. To help them in their own quests.

Perhaps.

Willy Boy knew they had a week ahead to play, to eat, to drink, to find a woman who didn't say he was too young. They would eat and sleep and enjoy themselves. Then in a week he would decide what they would do.

Whatever it was, he knew that he wanted to keep the Willy Boy Gang together, keep as many of the men as he could. They had forged a talented and working group of men into a deadly force. They could take what they wanted.

Willy Boy grinned and went to sleep. He knew that there was going to be more heard from the Willy Boy Gang. He was certain of it, and that made him grin even broader.